nd Three Vagabond Three Vagabond Three Vagabond Three V

Surviving

Allan Massie

Vagabond Voices
Sulaisiadar 'san Rudha

First published in June 2009 by
Vagabond Voices Publishing Ltd.
3 Sulaisiadar
An Rubha
Eilean Leòdhais / Isle of Lewis
Alba / Scotland HS2 0PU

ISBN 978-0-9560560-2-3

Printed and bound by Thomson Litho, East Kilbride

For further information on Vagabond Voices, visit our website www.vagabondvoices.co.uk

First, for Alison, as ever;
then for Damian, who has been there.

The ancients made much of the fact that the self is a mystery, but then every other living thing is a mystery, and it is much more difficult to peer into them than into one's own self (Gli antichi facevano un gran caso del fatto che il proprio io è un mistero. Ma anche ogni altra cosa vivente è un mistero e l'accesso ad essa è ben più difficile che al proprio essere) – Italo Svevo, *Soggiorno Londinese*

I

"You're mad," Belinda said, "you really are, out of your head."

"If you say so. You're the authority. But I don't think I am." There was no hostility, scarcely even sharpness, in Kate Sturzo's tone when she said, "You're the authority." They were good friends, could speak frankly to each other. There were secrets of course – when aren't there? – things either would prefer to keep to herself. Nevertheless …

As usual they had met in the little bar of no character in the Via Napoli half an hour or so before the other members of the group would appear. They valued this time together, it had become a ritual, and therefore comforting, even though they might also meet for a leisurely lunch some day during the week. But Kate had been in England the last two months, and now, returned, presented her with the news which prompted Belinda to say, "You're mad. You really are out of your head."

"I don't think I'm mad. I think it's interesting. He's interesting."

"He's a murderer, yes? – a killer, and you've invited him here, actually to stay with you in your apartment, and you say you're not mad. My poor sweet, you're raving."

"It was the little cough, you know, set me wondering."

"What little cough?" Belinda opened her blue-grey eyes very wide. She sipped her camomile tea and said again, "what little cough?"

"In court. During his trial. You do know, don't you, he was acquitted, all three were acquitted? When he was being cross-examined. He gave this little cough, really a clearing of the throat, before answering. It was

1

sort of modest, polite, rather sweet. He cupped his hand over his mouth. A nice well brought-up boy, I thought."

"So," Belinda said, "on account of this little cough you concluded he was all right, not a murderer."

"The jury came to that conclusion. Not guilty. Of course they had doubts, you could see that. I have doubts myself. But that's not the point. He's interesting, as a specimen if you like."

"And dangerous. Obviously."

"Maybe yes, maybe no. I talked to his mother. At some length, you know. A very nice woman. And I do have some experience."

That was true. They had both had some experience. They wouldn't have found themselves where they were now otherwise. Belinda was fifty, though she didn't look it, except for the crow's feet. Kate was five years younger. Her last book, an international best-seller – "good-seller, really", she said – had been the study of a very respectable and successful Belgian industrialist, accused in old age of long-ago war crimes, and found guilty. He was a genial fellow, known for his lavish gifts to charities. In the book Kate made his charm abundantly evident. It had pleased him, even though it exposed his crimes more fully than had been done at his trial. He had written of his admiration from the nursing-home to which he had been transferred from prison a few days after being sentenced to confinement for life.

"Oh, he was a charmer," Kate would say, to irritate people.

"Not just to irritate them," she told Belinda, "to open their eyes."

"To open their eyes ..." Belinda couldn't argue with that, not as a proposition. It was, deep down, what they were there for, what AA was all about: opening your eyes to the reality of your condition; hence acceptance. She knew what she should say. "You're a recovering alcoholic. You mustn't invite unnecessary stress. And this boy ..." It was no good. Kate knew the lines as well as she did, and had made her decision. They wouldn't talk about it at the meeting.

Others began to arrive. In recent weeks, meetings had been sparsely attended. Sometimes there had been more visitors to Rome than residents, regulars. They had debated, a couple of years back, whether meetings should be discontinued in August when most who could left the city. But Sol had insisted there must be meetings. Tourists who were in AA needed somewhere they could turn to. People left in the city were lonely, vulnerable. Now, regular members of the group were returning from the seaside or the mountains, or from visiting their families in other countries. There would be stories about the parents who couldn't believe that one little drink could do any damage, about the brothers and sisters and old friends whose own careless drinking provoked resentment, and so temptation.

Bridget and Tomaso showed up. Bridget was tense and silent. She hated meetings. She hated being an alcoholic. Tomaso accompanied her every week because he didn't trust her to make it on her own. There were few things he let her do out of his sight. In his sight much was permitted, like cooking and laying the table and clearing it and stacking the dishwasher. And paying the bills. He trusted her with that, while he stretched out in a chair. Tomaso was a film director, nominally. Before marrying Belinda he had worked, occasionally, at Cinecittà. Now Bridget, with her Trust Fund, occupied all his attention. She had only the income from the Trust; she couldn't dispose of any capital. So Tomaso was careful with her money, and saved where he could. Before they got together, Bridget had lived way beyond her income. Now her expenditure was small. Tomaso was however always very well-dressed.

"You've been in the mountains?" Belinda said.

"There's a lake. I swam every day."

Bridget spoke in a whisper. There was now scarcely any American left in her voice. Tomaso began to dilate on the beauty of the mountains, the healthy life they led there, how good it was for Bridget. He spoke as if she was a prize animal he was grooming for show. But he wasn't comfortable with Belinda. When they first met he had made a pass at her. "Oh no," she had said, "I don't think so, really."

Stephen and Erik came into the bar. Stephen smiled at Belinda and gave a little shake of the head to indicate that he would rather not come to their table since Tomaso was there. He ordered an espresso and a Coca-Cola at the *cassa,* and took Erik's arm just below his flowered short-sleeved shirt, between his thumb and forefinger, and guided him to the bar. Erik looked over his shoulder, and flashed Belinda a smile.

Kate said to Belinda: "I really don't fancy him in case that's what you're thinking. Not at all. I just want to know all about him ..."

"Can we have a word afterwards?" Stephen said to Belinda as they crossed the street to the hall of the American Episcopalian church where the meeting was held. "I'm in a bit of a state."

Belinda watched him as they settled. They had said the Serenity prayer, but it hadn't made Stephen serene. He chain-smoked, often stubbing out his Player's cigarettes before they were half-way through. She wondered if he was going to confess to a slip, but he didn't offer to speak.

Sol welcomed them back. He talked about his family holiday on Ischia, and of how he had thought during it of earlier family holidays on the Connecticut coast which had resulted in disaster. It was good to be not drinking, he said, and to know that his wife and daughters were free of anxiety. It was good to be able to go and do things on his own without carrying with him a picture of the apprehension on Amelia's face as he took off. These were among the solid rewards of sobriety, he said – convincingly.

A newcomer, a thickset man in the corner of the room, took a *toscano* cigar from his mouth, and said, "My name's Tom and I'm an alcoholic. I haven't had a drink for seven years, and I still don't like it. I still get twitchy come Martini time. But it's good to be able to be here. I've been in AA off and on and I have to confess that the stuff about handing things over to a higher power still grates. I'm too proud, I suppose. I know you're meant to get rid of pride, but I find that hard. It's the way I was brought up. Take pride in yourself, they used to say. Now I take pride in my sobriety, but I never do more than cling to it. That's all I've got to say. I'll be in Rome for a few months and I'm glad to have found you and to be here."

"We're glad to have you with us, Tom," Sol said. "I guess we each have to handle the problem of pride in our own way. It's a tough one. I used to have a stupid pride when I was drinking. I was even proud of my hangovers being worse than anyone else's ..."

Fergus began to speak. Belinda didn't listen. It was a long time since she had listened to Fergus who always had the same thing to say. It began with an encounter in a bar ... She watched Stephen instead. He was really twitchy. Then she let her eyes turn to Erik who was sitting some way apart from Stephen. His mouth hung a little open and a fringe of dyed blond hair fell over his left eye. He was concentrating on Fergus as if what Fergus said mattered. She reproached herself; maybe it did, to Erik.

5

"So this time I've learned my lesson," Fergus said. "I understand at last why I drink."

"That's good, Fergus," Sol said, "but it's not taking that first drink that's important. Knowing why you drink doesn't matter that much."

"Oh but I think it does," Lotte said. "My name's Lotte and I'm an alcoholic, and I didn't get settled into sobriety till I understood what I was running away from when I took a drink. And I did often." She laughed. "It was myself, you see. I was running away from the woman I had become. So I had to change myself to stop running away from myself. That is important, I think. It is what you must do, Fergus."

She treated the company to a smile. Belinda was embarrassed because Lotte embarrassed her.

Erik said, "I think that's awfully true what Lotte says. Oh, I'm sorry ... my name's Erik and I'm an alcoholic. I just know I was running away from myself when I drank. Sometimes I think I'm still running."

"Then slow down, Erik," Sol said. "But you're doing well. We all like to see you doing so well."

Now Mike made to speak, but Sol interrupted him to ask if he'd had a drink today. "Just a couple," Mike said.

"Then I'm sorry, Mike. You can listen. We're glad to have you here. But you can't speak."

"Oh hell," Mike said, "it's my wife, you see, Meg, she understands me, I can't take it ..."

Then you have to leave her, was what Belinda thought, if you can't take it without drinking. But maybe if you weren't drinking, you could take even being understood.

But she didn't know about that, she really didn't. She thought: Mike still plays the risk game. So does Kate, with this boy. Me, I've contracted out. I hope so anyway. I really do hope so.

II

"Erik's off to a party," Stephen said. "I tried to talk him out of it, but he wouldn't listen." They had walked up Via Nazionale and were sitting outside a café in the gallery that ran round that side of Piazza Esedra. It wasn't a place Belinda cared for, too near the railway station; it stopped, to her mind, just short of being sleazy. But tonight most of the people sitting there were tourists, all weary.

It was still hot in the velvet petrol-scented air of the city in this first week of September. With October, it was her favourite Roman month, but she would rather have been in another café and another square. They ate ice creams and drank coffee.

"So what is it?" she said.

"What is it? Hopeless."

She thought, not for the first time, you really should not be here, Stephen; you should have a parish with an Early English church in some nice town in the West Country, or Suffolk where there would be comfortable ladies of my age and upwards who would make much of you. But perhaps there were no longer such parishes, or, indeed, such ladies; she didn't know.

"Is it Erik?" she said.

"I'm crazy about him. At least I think I am." His voice floated Anglicanly high, attracting the attention of an English family two tables away. "And now he says he doesn't think he is gay at all. Can you imagine? It's a girl who's invited him to this party, an American girl we met at Porto Ercole, a college girl with a baby voice. It's making me wretched. I came so close tonight to taking a drink. I stared five minutes hard at a bottle of grappa ..."

"But you didn't. You didn't take one ..."

7

Chapter Two

"No ... but I might have, I all but did."

"You can't expect the young to be faithful," Belinda said. "You're forty, Stephen."

"Thirty-nine."

"And Erik's what? Nineteen?"

Stephen left her. She tried to persuade him to go home, or come to her place, stay the night, better for him, the state he was in, but no, he got to his feet, dropped a ten thousand lira note on the table, and left, his long thin legs moving clumsily as if they would lead him to knock against the tables between which he steered, in the direction of the railway station. It wasn't good. She called the waiter and paid the bill.

She walked down the long hill, her shoulder bag swinging. She had no fear of it being snatched. She had lived a long time now, fifteen years, in Rome, and never been the victim of bag-snatchers, not even in her drinking days. It was all a matter of the pace at which you walked: too quick and you were marked out as game, an anxious tourist.

She passed Trajan's column and market, and crossed the road to walk along the Corso side of Piazza Venezia. She turned left into the Piazza del Gesù, and made her way through the little streets and into Piazza Mattei, pausing there as she always did to run her fingers along the damp thigh of one of the stone boys holding tortoises to drink at this, her favourite fountain, and then into the old ghetto where she had an apartment. It was on the fourth floor and there was no lift.

Stephen and Kate, she thought. Stephen comes to me with a trouble which is the inescapable consequence of his nature, and Kate comes to me with what may be the equally inescapable consequence of hers, but which she does not recognise as trouble.

The cats came to meet her, mewing. They leaped on to the kitchen table to be stroked. They were Persians, brother and sister, and once, man and wife, till, reluctantly, she had the female neutered. She couldn't bring herself to have that done to Benito also.

She gave them some tuna from the fridge, and took a bottle of mineral water and a glass and went out to her little terrace from which she could see, over rooftops, the black pines on Monteverde. She sat on a basketwork chair and sipped the water, and smoked.

"I've got to know more," she thought, and thought of Kate eager for the visit of this boy who was, or almost certainly was, a murderer, even if he had been acquitted, for insufficient evidence as she remembered.

Her mobile rang. Kate.

"Are you all right? You're not worrying about me? I do know what I'm doing. OK?"

"Fine, take your word. What's the boy's name? I forget."

"Why do you want to know?"

"It irritates me, forgetting things. No other reason."

"I don't know, you think I'm off my head, don't you? You think it's dangerous. He's called Gary. Gary Kelly. Ordinary name for an ordinary boy."

"If he's so ordinary, why're you so interested?"

III

How did Belinda get through the day? The question was occasionally raised. Maura, brisk successful barrister and second wife of Kenneth Leslie, brother-in-law of Belinda's sister Fiona, said more than once that she had never known anyone do less. "I'm not saying I don't like her," she said, "I'm not even criticizing. It just amazes me, that's all."

"Oh she does this and that, I suppose," Kenneth said, "but slowly."

"If you say so. I'm glad we're not expected to stay with her, that's all. Not with those cats and no lift."

Belinda had never been a career-girl, deterred by her mother's example and urging. She had always been an onlooker. That was perhaps why none of her three marriages had lasted. The first didn't count. She could scarcely even remember it. When Kenneth told her that that husband, Oswald, was now a figure of some influence in the New Labour government, she opened her eyes wide, a mannerism dating from her lovely youth.

"I never think of Oswald, you know."

"But you do know he's a Life Peer, don't you, and though he's not in the Cabinet, has more say than most who are there."

"Poor Oswald."

Kenneth smiled. Belinda couldn't credit that he was himself a political journalist writing elegantly for a weekly that valued, though did not always recognise, elegance. Nevertheless she did sometimes remember it. That was why, coming in from the terrace, in the middle of the night, she had sent him a fax asking if he would be a lamb and look out press reports of Gary Kelly's trial, and anything else relating to the murder. "Sorry to bother you," she added, but didn't trouble to explain why she wanted the information.

It was Giuseppe, her third husband, who had installed the fax. He had gone on to e-mail before he left her. So the fax remained in the apartment. She used it to communicate with her broker.

She went down to the bar for her coffee. Seeing her step out of the already hot sun into cool shade, Aldo, without need of instruction, prepared an espresso and a cappuccino. His mother, heavy in black at the *cassa*, called out morning greetings and, instead of ringing up on the till, made a little mark in a book. Belinda paid them 50,000 lira in advance and they let her know when the money was exhausted. Kate disapproved of the manner in which Belinda organised her finances, in the bar, at the grocer's along the street, and at the fruit and vegetable stall in Campo de' Fiori.

"It's immoral," she said. "You invite them to cheat you."

"Oh I'm sure they don't."

Maybe they think I'm mad, she thought, but I don't think that either. If you trust people they don't cheat you, not ordinary people. Her broker might cheat her, but not Aldo or Signora Patruzzi, or Rico the grocer, or the old ladies Isabella and Lucia in the market. But Kate's trust – her apparent trust – in this boy disturbed her.

She drank her coffee and, as she often did, walked by way of the side streets and then across the Corso Vittorio Emmanuele, to the church of St Louis of France, to spend twenty minutes before the three Caravaggios there which depict the calling of St Matthew, St Matthew receiving help from an angel in the writing of his gospel, and then his martyrdom. Alone of the Apostles, St Matthew gave up wealth to follow Christ;

as a tax collector he had been on to a good racket. He did so reluctantly, if Caravaggio had got it right. And he must have, she thought. You can see that the pretty boy in the fine clothes and the hat with the big feather thinks Christ's call crazy.

The martyrdom panel always puzzled her. That was why she kept returning. Why is the magnificently muscled killer with the sword naked but for a loincloth? And why are there three or four all but naked boys and men in the painting? The one in the foreground has his buttocks bare. He is shrinking behind an equally young companion who is, one suspects, just as naked. Is the saint being murdered in a brothel? Has he come there to denounce immorality? Or has he come as a patron, and is the so-called martyrdom no more than a quarrel about the reckoning? Despite the swirls of draperies and the straining of muscles, the scene is strangely frozen. But perhaps, Belinda thought, not for the first time, that is what the moment of murder is like. Caravaggio would know, even though he wasn't yet a murderer when he painted St Matthew. But he would have seen murders, she'd no doubt of that, in the streets around where they both lived.

She lit a candle, though she had never accustomed herself happily to the replacement of real flickering candles by an electric device, and though she never told herself who she was lighting the candle for. It was just something you did, like stuffing a 5,000 note into an alms-box for the poor of the parish.

She crossed Piazza Navona which no longer seemed part of everyday Roman life as it had been when she first knew the city, and came into little Piazza Pasquino. She went into the tobacconist to buy cigarettes and was disappointed to find only the old man, the licensee there, and not his grandson, Mario. But the old man was courteous and the exchange of some insignificant sentences felt good. She left the shop feeling cheerful.

A tall man with broad shoulders, a bit hunched, and grey hair rather too long, was standing in front of the little statue of Pasquino, reading the notice affixed to it. He half-turned and she recognised him as Tom, from last night's meeting.

He was wearing a crumpled cotton suit, biscuit-coloured and with a few stains. There was the stump of a *toscano* in the right corner of his mouth, and he carried a soft straw hat. Seeing her, he made a flapping gesture with the hat as if to suggest that he would have removed it from his head if it had happened to be there, took the cigar from his mouth, and said, "You were at the meeting, weren't you? Maybe you remember me saying something?"

"Of course. Tom, isn't it? I'm Belinda. I almost never speak at meetings."

"I nearly always do. It's a bad habit. People rarely like what I say. They prefer happiness and optimism. That's my experience anyway."

"It's natural," she said. "We go to the meetings to be encouraged."

"I know. I should keep my mouth shut. But somehow I don't seem able to." Belinda wasn't sure whether he was laughing at her or at himself.

"You're here for some months, I think you said."

"Aim to be. I used to live here. When I was prosperous. In the Seventies."

"We must have just missed each other."

"Sad, eh?"

He smiled again, this time without removing the cigar. It had gone out, the way *toscani* do, and he put a match to it.

"This piazza," he said. "There used to be a *vinaio* over there, with a few tables in the back room. I used to drink in it, with an English Augustinian. I think it was where that restaurant is, but I can't be sure. Good times. Or I thought so then."

"A lot of these old *vinai* are restaurants now. Better for people like us, maybe."

"Maybe, but sad. Seen this notice? I always come to Pasquino soon as I'm back."

"That one's been there for a bit," she said. "Or perhaps it comes and goes."

In loosely rhyming couplets, the author of the *pasquinata* called for a new inquiry into the murder, now more than twenty years ago, of the poet and film director, Pasolini. He denounced a cover-up at ministerial level and accused the secret services of complicity in the killing.

"Could be something in it," Tom Durward said.

"Oh I don't know. There's nothing that Romans love better than murder and conspiracy."

"Don't we all. What about lunch?"

"It's a bit early. It's not twelve o'clock. Are you jet-lagged or something?"

"Just hungry. I'm never much good at breakfast."

"Well," she said, "if you can bear with me while I do some shopping in the market."

"Happy to ..."

They ate at a restaurant in the shadow of Pompey's theatre.

"Hope this place is all right," Tom said. "I used to eat here often. Now I've reached the stage or rather age at which there's no pleasure like nostalgia. Sometimes I think, no pleasure but nostalgia."

"It's all right," she said, "and I do know what you mean."

They ordered: *spaghetti alle vongole* for Tom, a salad of mozzarella and tomato for Belinda, with veal for both to follow. They drank mineral water. Tom crumbled bread. "Do you like AA?"

"Not a lot," she said, "but I need it."

"Yes," he said, "but enthusiasts depress me. You know, the ones who insist that we're special people. As if we were Calvin's Elect, for Christ sake."

"Calvin? Are you a Scot?"

"Way back. If I call myself anything, which I don't, then I call myself a Scot. But I prefer Bogey's reply to that sort of question in *Casablanca.* 'I'm a drunkard'."

"To which the answer," she said, "is: that makes you a citizen of the world."

"Which is no better. Has Bridget been coming to AA long?"

"Five years, I think. You know her then?"

"Of old. She once clawed my face open. She was a real street-fighter in her drinking days. But you probably know that. I guess Tomaso has saved her life."

"It's still an unhappy one," Belinda said.

"And how do you see yours?"

It was the kind of question she couldn't abide. And this Tom hadn't earned the right, which indeed nobody had, to ask it. She lit a cigarette, Gitanes with no filter.

"I don't ask myself that sort of question. So I can't answer when it's put to me."

"Intruding, am I? Sol asked me to tell my story at next week's meeting. Should I?"

"Probably. Up to you of course. Someone might benefit."

"But not you?"

He took some bread and mopped up the olive oil and veal juices on his plate. "What did you do this morning?" he said.

"Not a lot, went to look at the Caravaggios in the French church. I quite often do that."

"Used to be keen on painting," he said. "That's gone. Years since I was in a gallery, or a church. Pasolini talked about making a film about Caravaggio. I looked at a lot of them about then."

"You knew him then?"

"Not well. I was in the business in those days. Script-writer. Script-doctor too. But not well. I wasn't queer and I wasn't left-wing. I thought he was a phoney. Maybe he thought me one too. I've more sympathy with him now than I had then. Today's world's rather horrible, isn't it? You know there really might be something in these allegations on old Pasquino."

"Rome's full of conspiracy theorists," Belinda said. "It's more likely surely that it happened the way it was represented, that he picked up this poor boy, or boys, and they didn't like what he suggested. Or they just went too far roughing him up. Or it was robbery with violence, I don't know."

"Oh sure, it's more likely. I just said there might be something in the allegations. There were all sorts of odd things going on here then. Shall we have coffee, or do you want fruit or cheese?"

"No," she said, "coffee's just right."

Back in the apartment the table on which the fax machine stood was covered with a tumbled ream of paper. Kenneth had certainly responded. She wasn't sure now that she wanted to know. The feeling would pass, but ... She took a glass of mineral water from the bottle in the fridge and went through to her bedroom. She undressed but for her knickers and lay down. She slept badly at night but well in the afternoon. The cats came to join her.

Tom Durward had said he would sit in a bar with a book.

"I've a couple of dozen Maigrets in my book-bag. There's no comfort-reading like Maigret. Who was that twitchy guy at the meeting? Looked like a Church of England vicar."

"Stephen? He is a Church of England vicar, or was. He doesn't have a charge now. I'm not sure what he does have."

Tom Durward nodded. He took a *toscano* from his inside breast-pocket, and a cigar-cutter from his side-pocket, and clipped the cigar in half. He lit it and drew the smoke in. "I just wondered if I knew him," he said. "Nervy, isn't he?"

IV

Kate Sturzo was brisk in the morning, her time of day. She woke at 6.30, got up at once, had a glass of fresh-squeezed orange juice, showered, ate cereal and dried figs, and was at her desk by 7.15. In summer she wore shorts and a T-shirt for morning work, in winter a tracksuit. It was still warm enough to be summer.

In three hours she wrote 1,500 words of a paper she was due to give at a conference in Geneva in October. The title was "The Dislocation of Conscience". She started with a sub-title, "A Study in Criminal Mentality". That was what had been suggested to her. But she didn't like it. The phrase "criminal mentality" ... She read over what she had written. It didn't satisfy her, rang false. Would listening to Gary Kelly disturb the line she was taking?

Criminality, she thought, is self-programming, just as alcoholism is. Nobody is programmed a criminal by outside agencies. But could criminal behaviour be the making of a better person, like alcoholism?

Her own alcoholism had taken her by surprise. There was no family history and nothing in her life till she was well over thirty to suggest she would have trouble with booze. It had, as it were, ambushed her.

She had been brought up with wine as a part of everyday life, but not an important part. Her parents, second-generation Italian-Scots, had a grocer's shop with ice-cream parlour attached in Aberdeen. There was a flask of wine on the table at mealtimes, but it was rarely emptied. Giulio and Maria were serious people; they had done well, the shop flourished. When the supermarkets threatened the business, they moved upmarket, converting it to a high-class delicatessen. People came from all over the county to buy their coffee, cheese, prosciutto, salami and Italian wine.

They had restricted themselves to three children. Kate supposed they had practised birth control, disobeying the Church despite Maria's devout faith. Kate was the eldest, Caterina till she went to University in Glasgow. Pepe had gone into the business, making it still more expensive, more exclusive, more successful. Marco worked for an oil company; he too had now dropped the Italian form of his name. When they were young, Maria had taken them all, several summers in succession, to Italy, to maintain a family connection with a multiplicity of cousins. Now that she had lived years in Rome, Kate never saw them.

She had never married. She had settled there first on account of an affair with Angelo, a Professor of Law at the University. That was over some time ago. Angelo was now in politics, a member of parliament belonging to the Party of the Democratic Left, the reformed Communists.

Kate switched off her computer, and went through to her bedroom. She put on a cream-coloured dress with a broad red belt. She combed her hair. Her face was strong, the skin darker than it used to be, and there were lines running down from the corners of her mouth.

It was 11.15. She had an hour and a half before she was due to meet Mike. If he turned up. He had a habit of making a lunch date, as after the meeting the previous night, and then cutting it. Kate was Mike's sponsor in AA. She didn't much like him, told herself she might be a better sponsor for that reason. Affection interfered with judgement.

She checked her e-mail. She never did this before starting work for fear of distraction. There was confirmation of Gary Kelly's flight. He was arriving at noon the next day. There had been difficulty over his passport which the police were reluctant to return. She had had to speak to someone quite high up in the Home Office, and also to the barrister who had defended him, Reynard Yallett, an old acquaintance, now celebrated as a right-wing Rottweiler, much in demand for *Newsnight* and radio programmes.

Kate left the apartment, double-locking the door, and took the lift down. The porter was sweeping the hallway. She remembered to ask after his granddaughter who had been off school with chickenpox.

The leaves of the chestnut trees were still green, but dusty. Dust and spiders' webs lay on the oleanders. At the end of the street a group of boys were revving their motor bikes. They eyed her, obedient to their code, and one called out "Bella, bella" as she passed; routine.

She bought newspapers at the kiosk: *Il Messaggero, La Repubblica, Le Monde,* the *Frankfurter Allgemeine, Daily Telegraph* and *Herald Tribune.* She would read them intently, gut them, for information, not diversion.

Belinda couldn't understand why Kate chose to live in Parioli, a solidly, repressively, bourgeois district of dull nineteenth-century apartment blocks. It was its anonymity, its lack of character, the fact that nobody called it "interesting", that appealed to Kate; also the tree-lined avenues.

Waiting for Mike she worked her way through the newspapers. She took a pair of nail-scissors from her bag and cut out an article from the German paper about the fire-bombing of a hostel for Kurdish workers in Leipzig. *Le Monde* gave her a piece about the lax investigation into the murder of two Arab girls in the rue St-Denis.

She looked at her watch. Mike was late. Then he was there, sweating and looking rough.

"I bet you thought I wasn't coming. I thought I wasn't coming."

"It was your business whether you came or not."

"Do you mind if I have a drink?"

"I do, rather."

"Just the one necessary therapeutic drink," he said, and asked the waiter for a Fernet Branca and a beer.

"Peroni," he said, "there's nothing in Italian beer, Kate ..."

"That's an old line," she said. "You've used it too often. And haven't you been applying a spot of therapy already?"

"Hell," he said, "nothing serious."

When the waiter brought Mike his drinks, which he did with an expression on his face which indicated disapproval, as if he had had trouble with Mike before, Mike looked at the Fernet Branca for a couple of minutes, as if to say he could take it or leave it. But he took it, using both hands to lift the glass and hold it steady, and then gulped a third of the beer. He held himself very still, letting the liquor work, then stretched out his right hand and watched it. It shook only a little.

"Small town tremor," he said. "I was with Stephen. We were at that night bar off Via del Tritone. I'm not sure it was a good idea."

"I'm quite sure it wasn't," she said. "I'm not going to sit here and watch you drink, Mike. I don't have to do that."

"That's all right. If I was planning to go on, I wouldn't have kept our date. But I need help, Kate."

"Naturally," she said. "The question is: do you want it?"

"God," he said, "you're so good for me, Kate. If I can stick with you for a few hours, then I won't need a drink. I haven't been home and I can't face Meg till I'm off this jag."

"Have you phoned her?"

"Christ no."

"You should. But it's your life. Hers too of course."

"I think, Meg and me, we've come to the end, pretty near the end."

"Don't look to me for sympathy."

But she got him to come with her to a restaurant, and eat something. Ravioli, which is always easy, and some bread. When he had eaten most of it, he tried out a smile.

"You know what set me off?" he said. "I've got to tell you."

"You don't, you know. I'm not interested. It's irrelevant. I'm sure you told Stephen. More than once."

"But I do need to tell you. Really. I came home yesterday – if it was yesterday – for lunch and found Meg reading my manuscript, my novel. And you know what she said? She said, 'This is crap, Mike, total crap.' My wife. I don't need Meg to tell me my work's crap. The reviewers can do that if there are any reviewers. 'You used to have a talent,' she said, and let the pages of the typescript fall all over the floor. Sure, I used to have a talent, and who killed it, what killed it? Providing for her. I didn't say that. I didn't say anything, not out loud. I just turned and headed for the bar."

"Childish," Kate said. "Adolescent."

"You're so good for me. I wouldn't take that from anyone else. I didn't take it from Stephen."

"I suppose you hit him."

"What else was there to do?"

"I can think of a few things. It's not good, Mike, time you quit …"

"I know that. Don't think I don't know that. I've heard time called. 'Last orders, gentlemen, please' … Can we go to a movie?"

Kate paid the bill.

"Sometimes," Mike said, "I think I'm fucked. Stephen's fucked too. That little bitch Erik … God's jokes, that's what we are, and AA asks us to put our trust in him."

"Sometimes it works," Kate said. "For some people it works. For some it works all the time."

She crossed her fingers.

V

The telephone woke Belinda from a dream of her long-cold father ... They were in the November library of a dusty country house; rain smearing the windows. He had a tartan rug over his knees. He reached out for a packet of Goldflake and lit one, coughing. "I'm a done man, Bel," he said, "done up, down and out. That's our secret. Tell nobody because the news will reach your mother if you do. I'll deny her that ... satisfaction." He took her hand. His felt like dry bones covered with tissue paper.

She let the telephone ring. Fifteen times. Then it stopped. But it had killed sleep. She shook the dream off her. Benito stirred, extending claws. They dug but gently into the soft flesh of her upper arm. Strange dream, her poor father. She had been twelve when he died, not of cancer as the dream would have it. He had cut his throat in a Paris hotel, hard by the Gare du Nord. It was unnecessary. The case which so unnerved him had already collapsed.

Tea, she thought, pulling on a dressing-gown. Her legs, now reflected in the glass, were still good, better indeed than in her twenties. She looked at the reams of fax, and looked away; warmed the pot, a spoonful of Lapsang, kettle, let the tea rest three minutes; half-filled a Rockingham china cup. The tea was pale, straw-coloured, the scent finer than the taste. But she held the first mouthful a long time and allowed the lingering taste to remove the sourness of sleep and dream.

The telephone rang again. This time she answered. It was Erik.

"Stephen's not with you, is he?"

"No. Should he be?"

"I don't know. He wasn't home last night, so I guess I hoped he was still with you. It's not good. Can I come up and see you, Bel?"

"Up?"

"Yeah, I'm in the bar below, your bar. Please."

There was a no in her mind, but ...

"Give me ten minutes. I've been asleep, must have a shower. So, yes, ten minutes, all right?"

She looked a fright, she was sure of that.

Erik? From his first night at the meeting Mike took against him, denied him the right to be there. "Fucking phoney ... bumboy ..." Mike was drunk when he said that. No reason to suppose it didn't represent his true feelings, though Belinda had herself told too many lies when drinking and been told too many, countless, in reply, to put any trust in the line "in vino veritas". Veritas belonged the near side of vino.

She dried herself, removed the shower-cap, sprayed scent, dressed. She heard steps on the stairs, opened the door, offered her cheek, first one, then the other, held Erik just a moment by the shoulders, gave him a hug.

"Oh Belinda, I just can't think where he might be."

His voice was creamy, West-coast, a whine never far distant. But, as ever, to look at him was a pleasure, and to know that, no matter what Mike said, he was a disturbed boy. He might also be what Stephen in sad and angry moments said: selfish, shallow, unfaithful. But pretty. Very pretty.

Benito came and rubbed against the boy's white-jeaned legs, tail erect.

"Would you like some tea ...?"

"Oh thank you, that's exactly what I do need ..."

He flashed her that beach-boy smile.

"Was it a good party?" she said.

25

"Oh I knew he was jealous. I suppose he made a thing of it. But it was no big deal, not really."

"Stephen made it sound like one."

"Well, he would, wouldn't he? That's what bugs me. It's like I'm his possession. It's like we were married."

"Oh, not as bad as that, surely?" she said.

They took their tea out on to the terrace. Erik leaned against the wall. He had long legs, neat buttocks. His body looked very good to her when he was still. There was something gangling, uncoordinated in his movement, the way he threw out his right foot. She couldn't believe he had really ever had a serious ambition to be a dancer. He was just wrong for that.

"I'm not even a hundred per cent sure I'm a hundred per cent gay," he said, and smiled.

"Yes. That upset Stephen. But then is anybody?"

"Anybody what?"

"A hundred per cent anything."

Belinda had never been to bed with a woman, didn't like the idea. But what she felt for Kate and had felt for other women friends was more, in some respects and different ways, than she had felt for any of her husbands, or indeed lovers.

"Tell me about the girl."

"Oh her. She's nothing. Really, she's nothing."

"No?"

"No, honest. I'm really worried about Stephen. He might do anything."

"Oh I don't think so. Not anything, not really anything."

Was she already a little bored? Erik had that effect on her. And yet just looking at him was a pleasure.

He turned now, brushing that floppy lock of hair out of his eyes. The skin of his arms, bronzed against the white T-shirt, was soft, smooth, silky.

"Can we go look for him?" he said. "I can't do just nothing ... I feel I'm like some way responsible."

"Well perhaps, but it's time Stephen learned to cope with his emotions."

"Oh sure, I couldn't agree with you more."

Nevertheless she consented. There was no way not to.

"But first ring the apartment. He might be home now, you never know."

Erik dabbed out the number on his mobile.

"No answer. And no message. Just the standard no one to take your call."

"Well, you leave a message. Say you're with me and we're anxious. Let him know he's wanted."

"I guess he doesn't want to see me right now. He thinks I've behaved like a shit. But he doesn't own me. There are days I wish we'd never met."

"Very probably," she said and picked up her bag.

VI

Tom Durward brushed past back-packers in shorts as he emerged from the American Express offices in Piazza di Spagna. It was late afternoon. A little breeze had sprung up. There used to be, he had read, a breeze like this one that came at twilight into the city from the *campagna* carrying intimations of mortality – fanciful stuff? That was when the *campagna* was malarial, before it was drained. Was it Henry James who had remarked that breeze? Might be, sounded like him.

He turned right and, just before the Steps, paused at the house where, as he read, *Il poeta inglese Giovanni Keats, mente meravigliosa quanto precoce, morì in questa casa il 24 febbraio 1821 nel ventiseiesimo anno dell'età sua ...* in the twenty-sixth year of his life. It was more than twenty-six years since Durward had read a line of Keats, though the "Grecian Urn", the "Nightingale" and most of "Autumn" were lodged in his mind. Tom Lehrer: when Mozart was my age he'd been dead for years. How many years? Durward had lived, he calculated, almost two and a half times as long as Keats. If Keats had survived to Durward's present age, he'd have been able to read "In Memoriam" and, Durward thought, also "Maud".

It was a bad time of day, to be alone in a city ... not as bad as in an hour or two when the light began to fade, but bad nevertheless. Had he been foolish to return here, where so much of his past, thought to be buried, awaited – or threatened? – resurrection. And to return alone? But he was alone now wherever he was. "A man alone ain't got no fucking chance" – Harry Morgan's last thought, Hem's tribute to the solidarity of the Popular Front and the Republic, no enemies on the Left. Like hell, none. How was it early in the morning in Ketchum, Idaho? How do you like it now, gentlemen? That came a bit close, just a bit close. Sixty-two, wasn't he? That gave Durward eighteen months. When he was young and writing his first short stories for *The London Magazine,* Alan Ross had told him to fine himself for any echo of Hemingway. That was after he submitted a story about a Hemingway typecast hero and an Italian boxer. It wasn't a good story, and Ross had been right to refuse it. A dozen years later he'd sold it as a movie idea and scripted it. John Huston was to make it, then didn't.

Standing, hat in hand, on the lower steps of the great staircase, as if he was waiting for one of these boys with gold chains round the neck to approach him and with a luscious smile offer to introduce him to his sister – or was that another thought that dated him, belonging to lost time? – he saw Belinda crossing the piazza below him. He was tempted to call out, but didn't, not only because she was with the young faggy Yank from the meeting, but more because he was so in need of company and ashamed of the need. So he stood and watched as she slipped her right arm round the boy's slim waist, and he reciprocated with his left round hers and they moved, like a yoked pair, out of sight. Durward's longing followed them, against the breeze.

When he was young in Rome, he might, at this hour, have mounted the steps and made his way to a bar or pavement café on the Via Veneto where, then in Fellini-time, film people and beautiful people congregated. But it wasn't, he thought, like that now, and even if it had been, he wasn't now what he had been then. But what was? *Giovanni Keats, il poeta inglese* ... can you quote ten lines from any living *poeta inglese?* Not bloody likely.

At last, Durward moved, slowly and leaning heavily on his stick, along the Via del Babuino towards the Piazza del Popolo. He found a table outside Rosati's and ordered a pot of tea. He laid his Maigret on the table. He had read fifty pages earlier in the afternoon and was in no hurry to finish it. It was a late one but good. Maigret had been summoned to the apartment of a successful civil lawyer, near the Elysée Palace, by an anonymous letter which warned him that a murder would be committed there. The idea – the McGuffin – was absurd, its treatment compelling. Durward preferred his Maigret to be in a different, less moneyed, ambience; the canals of the Franco-Belgian border, a poor quarter of Paris or an Atlantic port. Nevertheless this was good. He wanted to postpone coming to the conclusion which, however, he was sure he could guess. Not that it mattered ...

"Tom Durward ..."

He looked up. At first he couldn't see who had addressed him, wasn't sure he was pleased to be recognised, even wondered if he had, not for the first time, imagined the speaking of his name. Then the woman at the table just behind his left ear, whom he could see only out of the corner of his eye, said, "and you don't remember me."

He stumbled to his feet and half-turned so that he could look at her properly.

He saw a woman, in or around her thirties, with *café-au-lait* skin, a nose that widened at the nostrils and was slightly tilted, and the sort of mouth often called generous. Her hair was piled high and she wore a dark cashmere jersey. He didn't think he had ever seen her before, and he didn't think she was the sort of woman he would forget.

"You really don't remember me. Well, that's a blow to my ego. Fortunately it's a substantial one, if buffeted."

"I'm sorry. You must think me stupid. And rude."

"You used to have much better manners," she quoted, "even when you were plastered. And you were, mostly."

She laughed and picked up what looked like a *negroni*.

"This is embarrassing," he said. He sat down on the vacant chair at her table. Seeing him do so, the waiter transferred his tea and his book.

"Embarrassing for you? What do you think it is for me?" She laughed again. "You bought me my first Martini."

"I did?"

"You did. In the Ritz it was."

That couldn't be right. He had always drunk gin rickeys in the Ritz, as far as he remembered.

"The Ritz in Paris."

"Oh, the Ritz in Paris. That must have been ... your first Martini?"

"It's too late for chivalry," she said. "More years ago than I care to think. 1975 to be exact."

1975? It was a year, one of a few around then, of which he recalled precisely nothing. He looked at her again. 1975? He must have been cradle-snatching.

"Did we ...?"

"We certainly did."

The smile she gave made her more certainly than ever under-age in 1975.

"This is awful. You said I was plastered mostly. I have to tell you that period of my life's a blank. Total amnesia."

"You were in a bad way, sure. Your nephew – Jamie? – had been drowned. You blamed yourself."

She must be real, unless she was a waking nightmare.

"I never knew," she said, "when you were making sense or not."

"This is awful," he said, again. "Least I can do is buy you a drink. *Negroni* is it? Looks like a *negroni*?"

"*Negroni*," she said.

He gave the order to the waiter.

"You're not drinking yourself?"

"I almost could. But no, I've retired. Been off it for years, seven actually."

"AA?"

"AA. How could you tell? What do you know about AA?"

"Seven years," she said. "People in AA always count, don't they? I've a husband. Not that he's ever lasted seven years. Seven weeks is a triumph. I've been to a few Al-Anon meetings myself. They're not my thing either, but I've a lot of respect. You must be secure, buying me a drink."

"Secure? I don't know as anybody's secure. What's your name?"

"Will that help you remember?"

"Doubt it," he said. "If I've forgotten someone who looks like you ... I just want a handle."

"I looked better then, in 1975," she said. "I guess we all did. It's Meg Baillie now, but that's not going to mean anything to you. I've been other things and Baillie only for five years, long years I have to say. But I used to be Meg Franklin."

"Franklin? You're Eddie's baby sister?"

"I should be offended you remember Eddie and not me ..."

"But I knew Eddie long before I fell apart. He used to talk about you."

"He talked about his baby sister? Come on."

"But he did."

Tom looked across the piazza. It was rush hour now. Cars jostled each other, horns blew, scooters nipped here and there. At the edge of the pavement, just in front of the tables, two scooters were parked. Boys and girls embraced. The girls who had been riding behind their boyfriends mounted one scooter and rode off, and the boys, calling after them, then clapped each other on the back and exchanged a comrade's punch to the chest. They got on the other scooter and zoomed away, bare-headed in defiance of the law. Durward, conscious of them, also saw a slim coffee-coloured boy naked but for a loincloth running through the surf of a Caribbean beach in a bad movie he himself had written ...

"Eddie," he said, "I haven't seen him in years. There was a long time I saw nobody. But I think of him quite often."

"Oh yes," she said, "so do I, often."

She looked away, across the piazza, to the pinetrees on the hill beyond.

"You're waiting for someone?" he said.

"Tell the truth I was waiting for anybody or nobody. Then I saw you and we got this conversation off on the wrong foot. Eddie's dead. I hadn't realised you didn't know. Though how the hell you couldn't have ..."

"I'm so sorry," he said. The words were no good. "I live out of things, see almost nobody, don't read obituaries ..."

"It was front page," she said, "not just obituaries. He was murdered. I never thought you could have not known. I nearly didn't speak to you when I recognised you; I nearly got up and walked away. If I'd known you didn't know, I would have."

33

The dance was out of her eyes. Tom Durward dug the nails of his thumbs hard into his forefingers.

"You'd better tell me everything."

"There's not much to tell. It's an old story, a nasty old story."

VII

"It's no good," Erik said. "He might be anywhere."

She understood. It had been impossible for him to return to Stephen's apartment and wait, and impossible for him to be by himself. But the futility of their quest was unimportant. He would be able to say, later: "I hunted everywhere for you, really everywhere. So did Belinda. We were so worried, so fucking worried."

"Is there anyone he might have gone to see, called on?"

"Oh I don't know. I just don't know. It's hopeless."

They had arrived back in the Via Condotti without her being aware of where they were going. She said, "We need a break. I know what you need. Poached eggs and strong Indian tea in Babington's."

"I've never been there."

"Oh but you should. Actually it's the sort of place that should be Stephen's. It's like a tea-room in an English cathedral city in a Hugh Walpole novel."

"I've never read him. I don't know that I've ever heard of him."

"No, I suppose not. I doted on his books when I was fourteen."

The waitress in black dress, lace apron and cap, served them. The eggs were beautifully cooked.

"Actually," Belinda said, "I don't suppose there are tea-rooms like this in English cathedral cities now. Everybody drinks lager, I'm told."

"Why did you come to live in Rome, Bel?"

"It just happened. What about you?"

"I was travelling and I met Stephen and well ... I guess I wanted to find myself."

"And have you done so?"

"No. Does anyone? Maybe it's just adolescent to be trying to do that. What do you think?"

Chapter Seven

She poured him another cup of tea.

"Oh," she said, "me. Tell me about the girl. That's part of your question, isn't it? Or did you think she might be the answer? In my experience other people never are. But that's just my experience, you understand."

"Stephen thinks I am for him. And I'm not, though it makes me feel good being wanted. Some of the time, and then it doesn't. He'd like to own me. Do you know what I'd like Belinda, just this minute? I'd like a drink. Rather urgently."

"I don't think that's a good idea."

"Oh sure, I know that. You forget, I spent even more years in junior Al-Anon than I have in AA itself. Because of my mother. So I know about it. But that doesn't alter the reality which is that I want a drink now, *subito*."

He smiled again, knowing chorus-boy, not sunny beach-boy this time.

"No," she said. "I think we should go home. You'll be better off there. And if Stephen doesn't find you at the apartment, he'll most probably ring me."

"OK. But do I want him to find me?"

Later in the evening, Erik began to weep. She felt first revulsion, then tenderness. She put her arms around him and held him. Having no words, she let her lips rest in his soft almond-scented hair. She rocked him in her arms and then led him, unresisting, to her bedroom. He let her undress him, all but knickers and socks. They lay together. He pressed his damp face against her. She wiped tears and licked her salty finger. He relaxed. When she was sure he slept, she traced the line of his lips, moving fingers between his mouth and hers. He moaned and, still asleep, freed a hand to let it lie against her cheek. She thought: I have paid my price to live with myself on the terms that I willed ...

VIII

Mike came on Stephen at the corner of the Corso. There was a shiny bruise under his eye where Mike had hit him. He was attracting glances from passers-by who kept their distance from him. Mike clapped him on the shoulder.

"You look bad," he said. "You can't stand here against a lamp post. You'll get in trouble. What you need is a beer. I'm sorry I hit you one."

"You hit me twice, once in the belly. I've been sick all day."

But he allowed Mike to guide him down the street, up the slope and into the broad piazza of the Holy Apostles.

"It's all right, don't need your arm," he said. He crossed himself as they passed the church.

"The Stuarts," he said.

"Stuarts?"

"James VIII & III, the last legitimate King born in the Palace of Whitehall's buried there. Did you know that?"

"Course I did," Mike said.

"Jacobite, always been a Jacobite, since I was a boy," Stephen said. "Did you mention beer?"

"What we need. What the human frame requires."

The *birreria* in the lane beyond the piazza was hot, noisy and crowded. But they found a table, safely in the corner where each could get his back to the wall. A large fat waiter, sweating hard, approached on waiter's flat feet, shook hands with Mike and laughed.

"You see, it's all right here, safe, they know me. *Sì, due scure grandi, Gianni, e poi, siamo vecchi amici, non è vero?*"

The waiter laughed again, laid a damp hand on Mike's shoulder, briefly, and hurried off. "That's the difference," Stephen said. "Difference between us. I feel safe in places where they don't know me ..."

They sat in silence till Gianni, with a flourish, put two tankards on the table, spilling only a little.

"Where they don't know me," Stephen said again.

"Thing is," Mike said, "necessity is, to find a place where they understand, understand the importance of a drunkard's life. Then you're all right. See?"

"Mike," Stephen said, "we're exiles from Eden. That's why life's a tragedy." Mike shook his head.

"Comedy," he said. "Tragi-comedy perhaps. But comedy, of errors, much ado about nothing, the Bard knew. So do I. I've been married three times, you know. Drink."

"To the Stuarts."

"OK, the Stuarts."

"Never been married," Stephen said. "Belinda's the only woman I could ever have married. But better not."

"Much better not. You could marry her, fag-hag, you know. But better not. Keep marriage off the menu. I know, speak from experience."

He signalled to Gianni for more beer.

"You were right to hit me. Brought me to my senses. Erik's no good for me, see that now."

"Little shit, told you. Must be hell being queer."

"What gets me is the little bitch saying he's not gay. After all I've done for him."

"Hell for you. That's life. You know Kate. She's my sponsor. Now she says she won't have time for me, she's got some boy – a murderer – coming to stay. Tragi-comedy, you see."

"Why?"

"Why what?"

"I don't know."

"You're right. We're both right. Nothing solves anything. Went to a movie with Kate, keep me sober she thought. But I slipped out for a pee, and here we are. Gianni!"

Later, several beers later, Mike said,

"Time to move. Time for a change, grappa is indicated, I think. Yes, grappa is definitely indicated."

"What does Kate want with a murderer?"

"Who can tell? Never been fucked by a murderer. Could be that. *Andiamo*. Find a low bar and drink grappa, that's the schedule ..."

IX

The telephone rang as Kate was about to leave for the airport.

"Reynard Yallett here. Your chicken's trussed and airborne. Thought you'd like to know."

"Thanks. Kind of you," she said.

Unlike you, she thought.

"Only just," he said. "He's afraid of flying. And of being recognised. And of being on his own. If I hadn't taken him to Heathrow, he wouldn't have got there. As it is, he doesn't know why he consented to your little experiment – and neither do I."

"Thank you," she said again.

"No need. I'm interested. I won't insult you by saying I hope you know what you've taken on. The boy's not as tough as he thinks he is, but he's a nasty, no question. You won't forget that, will you? Let me know how it goes. As I say, I'm interested. He has that effect. So of course do you. Might even give myself a weekend in Roma, see how it's going."

Kate thought: don't know why he's consented? For the same reason, Reynard Yallett, as you say yes to every journalist who wants to profile you, even though you know it's scheduled to be hostile. Vanity.

In Kate's experience almost nobody could refuse an invitation to talk about themselves, no matter what might come out.

Now the boy was beside her in the taxi, and looked away, out of the window. He was smaller (her height, five foot eight) and slighter than she remembered. His skin was pale and his fair hair cut short, not brutishly, but 1950s public-schoolboy style. He wore a thin black suit with big shoulders and a cream-coloured shirt open at the neck. No jewellery. He looked what she'd said to Belinda, a nice well brought-up boy. The little scar on his right cheek could, even might, have been the result of a sporting injury. His right forefinger picked at the skin of his left thumb. The hands were well-shaped, delicate, not working hands.

"We'll drop your things at the apartment, have lunch, and do the tourist stuff, just a bit."

The boy was in the spare room only a short time.

"Live here alone, do you?"

"Most of the time."

"I don't get it, having me here, with what you've been told. Isn't reasonable."

"No?"

"No. I'm not a poof, you know."

She all but said, what kind of a declaration is that? Refrained; irony was out. "Lunch," she said. "let's go."

The motor-bike boys whistled as they passed.

"You didn't ought to allow that. It's not respectful."

"It's just their way, means very little."

"You've got an Italian name, but you're English, aren't you?"

"Sort of, the way Kelly's Irish, yes?"

In the restaurant she talked about the city. His responses were few and short. He didn't know anything and was too proud to display his ignorance. He ate only half his plate of spaghetti.

"It's not good to eat a lot, slows you down."

He sipped his mineral water, looked at her directly for the first time.

"My mum was always on at me to eat more, but stuffing yourself's disgusting, I think."

"I liked your Mum, liked her a lot," Kate said.

41

"Yeah. She said you were all right. That's why I come. But Mr Yallett, he says to look out, says you'll twist me in circles."

"Do you believe him?"

"No. You might try."

"What about your dad, Gary? He walked out on you, didn't he? What do you feel about him?"

"Thought you said we weren't going to start working today. That question sounds like work to me."

"OK, we'll leave it. You're bright, aren't you, Gary?"

That was the impression she'd had when she saw him in court and then on the television. It was an unschooled intelligence, though in fact he hadn't dropped out of school completely till after GCSEs. Now, when she said, "You're bright, aren't you, Gary," the beginning of the smile he'd formed when he said, "That question sounds like work to me," was withdrawn. His face died on her. He lifted his hand to his mouth and gave a cough, that same demure little cough that had first attracted her attention, and looked beyond her to the open door.

"Coffee?" she said.

"Don't drink coffee."

"Don't you? I do."

X

Somebody once said, in her hearing, "all girls know ways to kill time, but Bel knows all the ways." She couldn't remember the speaker but she recognised the line as Scott Fitzgerald's, from his notebooks; notebooks and essays were what she read, she could no longer read novels and as for biography, that was all lies, in her opinion. She never knew if the speaker saw her as a Fitzgerald girl, or if it was just something that had come into his head and been spoken, the way most things are said, insignificantly.

If only it was true, she thought, but time is the one thing never killed, time is immortal, that's why it weighs so heavily upon us.

Erik slept beside her. He had twisted the sheet round the upper part of his body so that only the mop of hair, one temple and one eye were not hidden, but, lower, his left leg stretched out free of covering, and gleamed in the moonlight. Because of the blind there were alternating dark and light stripes across the leg.

She let the fingers of her left hand play on the boy's flat belly. Benito, on her pillow, thrust his face into hers demanding attention.

"Stephen doesn't like me, not really," Erik had said as she eased off his T-shirt. "That gets me down. He wants me but he doesn't like me, not really."

And maybe you're not likeable, she thought then, but now, doting, pushed away the sheet and leaned over and kissed him on the lips. He gave a little murmur and she stroked his cheek. There was just the faintest suggestion of bristle.

When they had returned to the apartment and found no message from Stephen on the answer-phone, and failed to get a reply when they rang his number, Erik said, "He's drinking and it's my fault."

Chapter Ten

"He's drinking and it's his choice. You know that."

"Do you think he's engineered this situation in order to have an excuse?"

"He's drinking because at this moment he'd rather drink than speak to you, rather drink than straighten things out. It's easier, it's always easier."

She sounded harsh, even to herself. Too bad, truth was harsh. Erik was charmed by her tone. He leaned over her chair and laid his hand on her shoulder. She turned and saw a gleam in his eye, as if a light switch had been touched. She passed her arm round his waist and drew him down upon her. They kissed. His tongue sought out hers. Then she pushed him away, got to her feet, smoothed her hair.

"Yes?" she said.

"I know what I wanted to know."

Well, perhaps, she thought now, or perhaps it was a line from a movie that felt right to him then. But whatever, they had, hours later after his tears, gone to bed and nearly made complete love. Now his hand rested between his legs which were spread out, and she slipped hers down the smooth body and pressed it. He gave a little moan. She thought of how Stephen must also, often, have heard that little moan, and of how he trusted her. "I hadn't looked for this again," she thought, "and it makes no sense, but ..." Benito purred in her ear and there was a plop as Elvira who had been lying at her feet jumped off the bed. It was all absurd; nevertheless. Voices were raised, quarrelling, from the street below.

Much later, with the first light of the new day sliding into the apartment, she got up, disturbing neither boy nor cat, and took a shower. Then wearing a butter-coloured, towelling gown which she had never liked, she made tea.

The tumble of fax-paper, undisturbed, waited for her.

What would Erik reply if, when the sun was full up, she said, "Let's go and get your things from Stephen's apartment?"

She tore the paper from the fax, sat at the kitchen table, and with a pair of scissors cut the roll into manageable sheets. Then she poured another cup, lit a cigarette and began to read.

Kenneth had done a good orderly professional job, assembling the material for which she had asked. It was presented as an almost coherent narrative.

XI

When Kate introduced the word "racist", Gary flushed.

"It's not like the way they said it was."

He wasn't easy. He had been more fluent on the television. He gave his little cough.

"Watch a lot of nature films, wildlife, you know, David Attenborough, that stuff. We're pack animals, aren't we? You've got to face it ..."

Then he fell silent, as if he couldn't.

She leaned forward and switched off the recorder, but he didn't relax.

"That'll do for today," she said. "We've made progress."

His tongue gave a quick lick to his lips. He stayed where he was, very still.

She thought, he doesn't know if I mean that. And if I do mean it, then he's beginning to wonder if he's surrendered anything of himself to me.

He had eyes that were always on the alert.

She thought: am I going to release him? No wonder Belinda tells me I must be mad.

She had seldom encountered so passive a subject. Her Belgian industrialist had loved to speak of himself, to explain his excellent reasons for acting as he had. He had wanted, after all these years, to be understood. But Gary was afraid of that, wasn't he?

When she asked him a direct question as for instance when she had asked, earlier in the session, "Why do you think Reynard Yallett took such an interest in your case?" she got only that grey look, indifferent as a city crowd.

"All right," she had said, "so how did he come to take your case?"

"It's his job, isn't it? What he does."

"But did you think he had some special interest?"

"Couldn't say."

"You wouldn't be a free man if he hadn't defended you in the way he did."

"Nothing they could prove."

Her nerves were frayed. She had to go to the meeting.

It came to her that the boy might defeat her; that she might extract nothing; that his moral nullity might even make sense.

"So what have you done with him?" Belinda said.

"I sent him to the cinema. Actually I stood by him till he was safely in. The Pasquino naturally. I can't imagine he'd have stayed in an Italian-language one. Though you never know."

"Are we going to be allowed to meet him?"

"If you like. If you like. I'm not getting anywhere yet"

"You will," Belinda said. "You will, I've every confidence in you."

"It's a hard shell," Kate said. "I've no idea what it contains."

"Mind you, I still think it's horrible and crazy."

"He's not horrible, you know, not really."

"Oh quite. I do understand that people can do horrible things and not be horrible themselves. Who was it said, 'We're all existentialists now'? Maybe he was right, whoever he was."

Tom Durward came into the bar.

"Do I have time for a coffee? I'm nervous. I wish I hadn't agreed to tell my story."

"We all want to hear it," Belinda said, "dying really, speaking for myself, can't wait ..."

XII

"My name's Tom and I'm an alcoholic. I've been dry for seven years and sober maybe for two. You all know the difference. Or maybe some of you don't. And maybe I'm kidding myself that I have felt the difference. I still kid myself, the same way I thought for years I fooled other people."

He paused to put a match to his *toscano*.

"I was a drunk for a long time before I was an alcoholic. I used to be quite happy being a drunk, admitting it. But not of course an alcoholic. I was lucky. I worked as a writer, mostly scripts for movies, and that's a trade where it's OK to be stewed as long as you deliver. And for a long time I did that, delivered. So I was fine. It wasn't so fine for my wives. I got through a couple in ten years. It was the women's fault that they weren't man enough for the job. I never saw things from their side, always my own. Anyway – some of you won't like this – I never had any difficulty finding another woman. So what the hell?

"Then my brother and his wife were killed in an air-crash, and I was left as guardian to their boy, Jamie. That should have sobered me up. I really cared and I was responsible for him. But I understood responsibility as providing, and I did that. So it was fine, even when I had minor goes of the DTs. I was OK. I was tough. The movies were still using me and I made more money than even I could spend.

"Then Jamie died. It was an accident. He was drowned in a lake at his school in England. So now guilt was added to self-pity – the self-pity had been there for years, though I didn't see that then. It was absurd. Here I was, the would-be great writer, with an unwritten novel in the Hemingway class, not writing it, but scripting epics of ancient Rome and all that sort of thing. But now I had

48

a real excuse to go right under: Jamie's death. I used it, oh how I used it. Nobody could blame me, could they? I was a drunk through excess of sensibility. So I drank to kill feeling. Undoubtedly it worked, but the feelings I was killing were decent ones.

"That went on for years. There are years of which I have no recollection whatsoever. I met one of them this week, a figure from those years. I'd made love to her and I had no memory of it.

"What do I remember of that time? Four o'clock in the morning, in hotel rooms, high up, with the night traffic moaning and the wet street below waiting for me to jump. But I never jumped and I still don't know why. There was never a four o'clock in the morning I didn't think of death.

"So there I was in the wilderness. There was no voice except my own and what I heard was, you can't go on.

"And I rang the AA helpline. I hated doing it. I hated the idea of myself doing it.

"The man who came to me was black, with a ridiculous goatee beard and a lisp. He was a jazz pianist and he looked at me and said, 'Time for you to come home, man.'

"I hated it. I hated him. I used all the arguments which I won't repeat because you will have used them yourselves. Some of you anyway.

"Then he said: 'Who told you you were beat, man?'

"I'd no answer. How could I have?

"But I fought. I went with him to meetings and listened to what was said, and growled and snapped like an old dog that's chained up. I'd come to a place where people presumed to understand me, which felt like an insult, so after the meeting I headed for a bar and drowned their understanding in Scotch.

Chapter Twelve

"I kept going back though. I couldn't not. Only this road offered me any hope and what I feared most was the final departure of hope. So I stuck around, arrogant and awkward, till somehow I came through. I can't say I've attained serenity. But I can live with myself now, without a drink.

"One thing I've learned."

Tom Durward paused and looked round the room and took a draw on his cigar.

"I'd got it all wrong. I thought I was fighting booze. But I wasn't. I was fighting myself, I was fighting the delusion that life had done the dirty on me. And that was all in my mind. I cheated life. It hadn't cheated me. 'Who told you you were beat, man?' That's a question you have to take both ways. When you do that, you're ready to come through.

"I don't think a lot of this is orthodox AA. I can't do the Twelve Steps. But I hope it says something to someone here. Thanks for listening."

XIII

Gary wasn't at the bar.

"I told him to come here. I even pointed it out to him. It's just round the corner from the cinema. The movie must be over by now."

Kate said all that, several times. She pushed her hair back, out of her eyes. She got up from the table and crossed the piazza to the fountain around which young men and boys were lounging, three or four of them perched on their scooters.

But of course Gary wasn't among them. She had gone to look only because movement was easier than sitting and waiting. She was like someone who steps into the road to look for a taxi that is expected, as if the act of leaving the house will exert influence and cause it to appear.

The air was heavy, fine weather departed. A gusty wind tossed paper and polystyrene cartons, cigarette ends, testimony of summer nights, about the piazza.

Erik leaned forward, brow smooth, to sip his Coca-Cola through a straw. Tom Durward drew on his cigar. Belinda let her fingers rest on the glass of camomile tea, said to Tom, "That was good, what you said."

He said, "There used to be a Neapolitan mastiff in this bar. It used to lie in the middle of the piazza."

"That was a long time ago."

"Of course it was. I once saw a lunatic pick it up and throw it over the bar."

Erik opened his eyes very wide. "He must've been strong, they're big dogs, like."

He doesn't believe Tom, Belinda thought. So he's being ironical or what he would think ironical. Or is he trying to interest Tom in him? As long as he's with me, if he really is with me, I'm going to be asking myself that sort of question.

Erik now looked away, his lips parted, and let his gaze wander round the piazza. He had hooked his right arm round the back of the chair, and his left dangled free, the fingers looking like they were floating.

Tom said, "This boy your friend's looking for ... I wasn't listening. Who is he? Her son or what?"

"Oh, what, very definitely. Not her patient exactly. You could say her case."

"Uh-huh, don't think I'll hang around. Take a stroll. I like that, in cities, at night. Don't sleep well. Nobody does after fifty, I suppose."

For a moment, having got to his feet, he hesitated, as if wondering whether he should lean down and kiss Belinda on the cheek. But instead he placed his right hand on hers which was resting on the table, placed it so lightly that she felt its weight but no pressure, picked up his stick and turned away. They watched him limp towards Via Lungaretta.

Erik said, "I was awfully impressed by his story. But he acted like I wasn't here. When I thanked him for it, he just looked straight through me."

"I think he resents telling his story," Belinda said.

"He could've refused."

"I rather think he would regard that as a sign of weakness."

A black dog of indeterminate breed sniffed round their table. Erik shifted his legs away from it.

He smiled at Belinda.

"I'm nervous," he said. "Not of the dog. It's just I don't know where we're at. You thought I was looking at that guy over there ..." Belinda turned to see a thirtyish Italian in white silk shirt open at the neck, dove-grey suit and loafers.

"So I was. He's gorgeous."

"I suppose he is ..."

Erik screwed up his face. For a moment he looked like her cat Benito.

"I read these faxes," he said. "While you were getting ready. They made me pretty nervous too. Does Kate know what she's playing with?"

"Oh I don't think it's a game. But I agree, I'm with you, of your mind entirely, it makes me nervous too."

She leaned forward and touched him on the cheek. He took hold of her hand and pressed her fingers to his lips.

"You do know you're free?" she said. "I make no demands," she lied.

Belinda knew that Kate, anxious, wanted to talk, but not with Erik there. Too bad; she wasn't going to send him away, dismiss him as of no account. She was being foolish, yes. Kate mattered to her in a way that Erik never would; and Kate was anxious. Again, yes, but the converse was true. Erik mattered, and she couldn't treat him as a child, which, being young, was how he would take a request that he leave them to talk. She could be selfish herself. She had once overheard someone say, "Have you ever known Bel do anything she didn't want to do, or not do anything she did?" That was true, or had been for a long time. And one reason she was close to Kate was that Kate was like her in this respect. So, usually, each knew not to demand too much of the other.

But Kate was making demands now, silent, urgent ones. The night turned smokey-violet. The piazza was thronged, people of all ages making what would be, except for the young, their last *passeggiata* of the evening.

A party of five settled themselves a couple of tables off. There was a girl with cropped black hair, in a red leather dress and sandals. She was very thin, but she had to be thin for that dress which was cut short showing the length of her thighs. A tall blond boy put a shawl round her shoulders.

"I've seen them before," Erik said. "I'm sure they're celebrities."

Kate lifted her arm and waved. Belinda followed her gaze across the piazza. A boy came towards them. He wore a black suit and pale shirt open at the collar.

"Where have you been? I was thinking you were lost."

He sat down without replying, turned expressionless eyes on Belinda, then glanced at Erik, and his tongue touched his thin lower lip.

"It's easy to get lost round here," Kate said.

"Went for a walk, film was crap."

The waiter approached.

"They can't make tea, can they? I'll have a Coke."

Kate made introductions.

"Pleased to meet you," Gary said, his mother's son, well brought-up.

Erik said, "What was the movie?"

Gary looked as if Erik was speaking a foreign language, and it was Kate gave the answer. "It's not such crap," Erik said, "least, I didn't think so."

Belinda, aware of his long legs shifting and his bare tanned arms, said, "Each to each."

Erik leaned towards her and spoke in a half-whisper.

"They can't be celebrities. They're looking at us. I think they're English."

The waiter brought Gary's coke. He touched the cold glass with his finger and looked over at the party who were looking at them.

"I don't like it here," he said to Kate. "Can we go?"

Without waiting for an answer, he got up and walked away, not looking back. Kate was flustered.

"I'd better ..." she said, "you don't mind, do you, Bel?"

"That's all right. I'll take care of this," Belinda said, meaning the bill.

Erik watched them out of the piazza.

"I'm sure he killed that boy. I just know he did."

Then a voice was raised from the English table, a bit thick with drink.

"Oh, come off it. You've seen him before, so it must've been on the telly and he must be an actor. There's more to life than telly, for fuck's sake, Lou."

"It's bizarre, sitting here with a murderer," Erik said. "I was watching him closely, see what I can use."

"Kate has her doubts."

"But have you? You don't, do you?"

"Oh, it's not in my line, my sweet."

"Excuse me, do you mind," the tall blond boy had come over, "that boy you were with. My girlfriend's sure she's seen him on the telly. She's sent me over to ask, hope you don't think it's rude. Eastenders she thinks, or it might have been Blind Date. Is she right?"

"Oh, I wouldn't know, she could be," Belinda said. "Blind Date seems more likely, whatever it is."

XIV

Tom Durward leaned over the parapet of the bridge. Reflections of street lights shimmered on the water. There was a Chinese proverb: the virtuous delight in mountains and hills, the wise in rivers and lakes. Like all proverbs it meant less than it pretended to. He had left Belinda and that boy in the piazza because he couldn't bear company, and now felt no better for being alone. He wished he hadn't told his story at the meeting, or had told it differently. He used Jamie, or the memory of Jamie, as dishonestly in sobriety as ever in his drinking years. At least he had said nothing of Paul, the black pianist, beyond reporting his words; nothing of how they had fallen out, of how Durward had let his malice work on Paul.

He rested his elbows on the parapet and relit his cigar.

Old Norman Douglas, dead years before Durward's first visit to Capri, asked, "Why prolong life, save to prolong pleasure?" Who was it used to quote that line to him?

At the far end of the bridge voices were raised in altercation. English altercations. Then he heard a slap, the sound of open palm on cheek, and saw the woman turn and walk away. She turned off the bridge and marched along the Lungotevere. Her companion watched her till she was out of sight, and, with long shambling motion, advanced towards Tom, and supported himself on the parapet.

"Did you see that?" he said, first in English, then haltingly in Italian.

"Couldn't miss it."

"She expects me to run after her. She's going to be disappointed."

"We all are, often."

"You're right there, too right. What do you say to a drink?"

"No."

"What do you mean?"

"I say no to a drink."

"There's no need to be like that."

"Oh but I think there is. In my case there is."

Back in his room in the Pensione San Giorgio, Tom stripped and showered. He let the cold water run over him and held his breath the time it takes to boil an egg after the water bubbles. Then he towelled himself hard and took a swig from the bottle of mineral water which was flat and tepid. When he was first in Rome, a lifetime ago, he had demanded San Pellegrino in restaurants (to go with the wine then of course), it being the only Italian water he had heard of, and had thought they were trying to palm him off with an inferior product when they gave him the only mineral water they kept there. He had made a fool of himself protesting. He lost his temper easily in those days.

Now he put on a sarong and a dressing-gown over it. He had slept in a sarong for thirty years, since working on a movie with an Eastern theme. He couldn't recall the name of the movie, but had no difficulty in picturing the Eurasian actress who had given him his first sarong. Her career hadn't come to much. She was so dumb, as the old line went, she fucked the writer. But Suzie Lo hadn't been dumb at all. She had fucked him because it pleased her, not for misplaced reasons of ambition. She was probably running a business in Hong Kong or Singapore now. She had been smart enough to leave him, even – or especially? – when he offered marriage. Image of her legs spread out, the colour of some spice, he couldn't name provoked remembered lust.

Chapter Fourteen

He snipped another *toscano*, removed the band in the Italian national colours, lit the cigar and settled at the little table which rocked when he placed his elbow on it. He opened his journal, at random. It was the nearest thing to serious writing he did now. "Stop that, be your age," he said, "serious writing ..."

When you live by yourself you get in the habit of making conversation with yourself. He read a note made some time ago:

> In East Germany, the Party tried to create a new specifically East German elite. They were brought together under the absurd slogan, *Greif zur Feder, Kumpel* (Grab your pen, mate). Young writers were encouraged to become involved in society by spending time in a factory or on a farm before writing about their true-to-life experiences ...

He couldn't think where he had got that from. *Greif zur Feder, Kumpel* wasn't – set aside the tone – such bad advice, not really "absurd" at all. What else could you say to a writer, what else worthwhile? And the true-to-life experience? It was like the sketch of the author on the back cover of an old Penguin: Hank Brockett has been deckhand, rodeo writer – no, rider – and insurance agent. As a young man, he ran guns for the IRA.

But what a sad business it is: excavation really.

So what else did he record in his journal? Well, he noted down, sometimes, what he remembered out of dreams, though he never retained them with the clarity some others claimed to. There rarely a narrative to follow.

But this, for example, two nights ago:

> There were earlier things, comings and goings, and then I was set on a long uphill march, through soft sand that came up to my ankles every stride. I wasn't the age I am now, I think I was adole-

scent. And an exile? Or in flight? I don't know. It was something to do with my sister. I had been cruel to her. Bullying or actual assault? Then I was back at school, in rugby kit, expecting to practise with my scrum-half partner Anthony. But he wouldn't pass me the ball. I was in disgrace. I was lying on a bed. My sister Louise came and stood beside it, and told me to get up. Anthony was with her. "You're going to be taught a lesson," one of them said. I was afraid; it was cold as a court of justice. I rose from the bed, affecting nonchalance. Then, in a surge of anger, I took Louise by the shoulders and pressed hard. "If anything happens to me, you'll regret it," I said. "You'll regret it for ever." I felt Anthony's eyes on me. They weren't their liquid brown. They were cruel as ice. "No," I said, "I didn't mean that, I really didn't mean that ..."

And I woke. Shaken and afraid. I listened to the World Service, and didn't sleep again.

XV

Discussing feelings wasn't in Belinda's line. Residual Calvinism restrained her. Class too; her grandmother Grace taught her that talk of emotions was self-indulgent vulgarity. You dealt with your own feelings, granted others the respect of leaving them to do the same. One of her great-aunts had turned to Moral Rearmament. Grace despised her sister-in-law's attempts at "sharing".

All this contributed to Belinda's reluctance to speak at AA meetings. She admitted AA was necessary for her; nevertheless could not overcome distaste for self-exposure. She understood why Tom Durward had not been able to stay with them in the piazza. This affinity pleased her. Really, these Americans with their passion for self-analysis. It wasn't grown-up.

Erik still slept, with the sheet again twisted round his upper body. She kissed him before slipping out of bed. His breath was milky.

Back in the apartment the night before, he had read again the reams of fax Kenneth had sent. Gary excited him. She disliked the thought.

The Calvinist conscience worked both ways. Her emotional reticence brought on self-reproach. Wasn't it merely another manifestation of her self-centredness? No intruders permitted in her private garden? So, two or three times a week, she forced herself to make a morning round of telephone calls to the other members of the group.

She called Sol first. That was always easy and short. They assured each other all was well, spoke briefly of last night's meeting. Yes. Tom had been impressive, hadn't he? Today she was tempted to speak of her anxiety concerning Kate; nevertheless didn't.

60

Usually she would then have called Kate herself. That was the enjoyable one. But she was reluctant, told herself the sun was too high, Kate might already be working with Gary, even if Belinda couldn't imagine how she could bring herself to do so.

She took her mobile out on to the terrace, lay back in a canvas chair and dialled Bridget's number.

"You weren't at the meeting. I was just hoping there's nothing wrong, that you're all right."

"All right? No." Bridget spoke on the telephone in a whisper, always. "But then I feel awful till I've done my exercises."

"Sorry, have I called too early?"

"No, it's fine. How are you yourself? All right?"

"As can be. I'll let you get on with your exercises then."

It wasn't what was said that mattered, just the act of making contact that reassured them all.

It was Tom Durward she wanted to speak to, but she had no number, didn't even know which hotel he was in. He probably preferred it that way. He would be sour with himself this morning. But it was a beautiful one, with just a touch of crispness, hint of autumn. She called Mike, dutifully. Meg answered.

"Oh it's you. No he's not here. I haven't seen the bugger for three days now, and do you know, that's fine by me. I don't give a damn. The second night I didn't sleep, but then this morning I said to myself, to hell with him, it's his life, if he chooses to shut me out, OK, I've had enough. I think I'll go shopping."

"What set him off this time? Do you know?"

"Don't know, don't care. Does it matter what set him off?"

Chapter Fifteen

"No, it never really matters, I know that. Any given reason is only an excuse."

"Too right, and I'm tired of excuses. I've had excuses."

"How are you yourself, Meg?"

"Oh fine, just fine. I might not go shopping, I might go to the beach. I'm fine."

"That's good," Belinda said, not believing her. "I've a notion Mike may be with Stephen. I'll try Stephen."

"It's up to you, include me out. But, say, was a guy called Tom Durward at your meeting?"

"Yes, indeed. You know him then?"

"Long time back. He was drunk when I knew him. But ... he was a friend of my brother Eddie, Eddie just adored him."

"I didn't know Eddie, remember."

"Poor Eddie."

"Mike'll turn up," Belinda said.

"I guess so. Too much to hope he won't."

"I'll ring Stephen, let you know if he's there. Bye for now."

But she didn't immediately call Stephen. She went down to the bar for her espresso and cappuccino, exchanged the nothings of the day with Aldo and Signora Petruzzi, felt better for it, stepped out into the street. Swifts that in Spring nested high up in the Teatro Marcello hurled themselves to and fro across the intense blue. The *scirocco*, to her surprise, had dispelled itself.

Back in the apartment Erik was stretched out in a chair on the terrace, a towel round his waist. He was reading one of Kenneth's fax sheets again, frowning. He looked almost ugly when he frowned; then he lifted his head and smiled. Kenneth had once told her, regarding himself in the mirror, that Plato had said there would have been no philosophy if there hadn't been so many beautiful boys in Athens. Well, she was no philosopher and she had never heard Erik say anything remotely interesting. What of that?

"Why are you looking at me like that?" he said.

"Never mind. I'm going to call Stephen. Are you here or not?"

The boy's mouth hung open for a moment. He got to his feet and turned away from her, leaning on his elbows on the terrace wall.

"I don't want ever to see him again."

"That's very sudden."

"No," he said, "it's just that I'm saying it suddenly."

"But I've got to call him and he's sure to ask if I know where you are. So what do I say? He does love you, remember."

"I don't want to be loved that way, not any longer."

"Oh dear. You were anxious, distressed, even about him when you came here."

"That was yesterday or the day before. You don't have to call him."

"Oh I think I do."

"Say what you like but keep me out of it."

"I don't know that I can. He may not be home of course."

XVI

"Think I'm some sort of specimen, don't you? Something you can pin to a page."

"That's not how I think of you, Gary."

"Then what are you doing with me? Why did you want me here?"

"You know the answer to that really, don't you?" Kate lit a cigarette. "Let's get back to where we were. To your father. How old were you when you realised that in his absences, he was in prison?"

"Wasn't a secret, ever. Where I come from ..."

"Yes?"

He frowned. When his brows came together he looked a different, responsible person. "Yes?" she said again, keeping impatience out of her voice.

"You don't understand. You can't understand. Where I come from, there's us and them, and you are one of them. Different, that's what, we're different. You want to know how I felt when I knew Dad was in prison. I felt big. I felt good."

"Because he was out of the way?"

"No, not that. Because it meant I was somebody. It's good to have your Dad a hard man. Gets you respect."

"That's important?"

"Course it is. Respect matters. When you get respect, you matter. I was twelve, maybe still eleven."

"And respected? Because of your Dad being in prison."

"Yes, that's right."

"What was he in for that time?"

She knew the answer of course. Joe Kelly was an enforcer. GBH. He had carved a shopkeeper who was slow to pay protection money, carved him to encourage the rest ... The only surprise was that he had been arrested and the trial had brought in a guilty verdict. But ... it didn't do to be soft, she had already heard that line from Gary. Was it pure chance however that the shopkeeper of whom he had made an example was a Pakistani?

"It was his job," Gary said. "Collecting like. He got longer because the guy he put the frighteners on was a Paki. Didn't matter to Dad what colour he was. He hadn't paid. See?"

"But you felt big because your Dad was in prison?"

"I've said that, haven't I?"

Kate stubbed out her cigarette and lit another.

"You smoke too much," Gary said. "That's your seventh since we started."

"Does it worry you?"

"Why should it? It's not healthy though. Woman like you should take care of herself."

"Your Mum smokes, doesn't she?"

"Used to hide her fags when I was a kid. Can we take a break? Cup of tea?"

Was she getting anywhere? She didn't know yet. He trusted nobody, except, maybe, his mother who went, I'm sure, straight out to buy another packet of cigarettes when she couldn't find the one which she knew he had hidden, or to beg a smoke from a neighbour. She would have been at one with her neighbours. Yes, I was right in thinking her a good woman.

"My Dad never laid a hand on me." Gary's voice followed her to the kitchen. "It was Mum used to give me a clip round the earhole."

Waiting for the kettle to boil Kate thought of an essay by Borges she had read. It was entitled "A Comment on August 23, 1944", the day of the liberation of Paris. Borges set himself to answer the question why even those Argentines who had been supporters of Hitler seemed excited by the news. And his answer was that nobody could live in Hell, could wish to live in Hell. He recalled another day, the one on which the Nazis marched into Paris, when an admirer of Germany and Hitler came to announce the news, adding that the Wehrmacht would soon be in London too, and Borges heard a whinny of fear below the chant of triumph.

And how, Kate thought as she spooned tea (Twining's Irish Breakfast) into the pot, did Borges account for this?

She couldn't remember his exact words though she had copied them into the common-place book she had kept since she was a child at school in Aberdeen, and Miss Fiddes, a dry spinster on the surface, whose soul was enflamed by a passion for literature – so that her life, seemingly confined between the frozen granite of the school buildings and the Thirties semi-detached bungalow in the suburbs which she shared with her war-widowed mother – was in the reality of her imagination a succession of dazzling images and wonderful journeys, had told the class that such a book would be "an everlasting treasure". They had sniggered and later imitated her precise way of saying this, but Kate at least had found that she spoke truth.

Borges then: he concluded that for Europeans and Americans – and Argentines were both – only one order was possible. It used to be called Rome and was now known as Western Culture. To be a Nazi, Borges thought, or to be playing the fierce barbarian, Viking, Tartar, conquistador, gaucho, Indian, was to try to deny the reality of this order, and was in the end unendurable. "Nazism," Borges wrote, "suffers from unreality like Erigena's Hell," since nobody, not even Hitler, nobody in the intimacy of his silent soul, can truly wish Hell to triumph. Even Hitler, Borges conjectured, sought defeat. Why else – this was Kate's gloss – his infatuation with *Götterdämmerung*?

And Gary, her little Nazi, for that is what he was inasmuch as he espoused nihilism, could she bring him to the point where confessing his uninhabitable world, he could enter into the reality of the sane?

She took the tea through to the work-room. The telephone rang.

"Reynard Yallett here ..."

"Yes?"

"Making progress with my little chicken?"

"Perhaps."

"Cautious, eh? I suppose he's with you."

"Yes," Kate said. "What do you want?"

"Always to the point, eh, Kate? Thought you'd like to know. I'm flying out to Rome this weekend. Can't keep away from your fascinating experiment."

"It's got nothing to do with you."

"After I set it up? That's not very nice. And another thing, there's a question going to be asked in the House, about how our chicken was returned his passport."

"There was no reason not to, no legal reason. You know that, you argued the bloody point."

"So I did. But the law and politics are clean different things. That journalist Trensshe has been stirring the pot. The Home Secretary is not amused. Trouble ahead."

"That's nonsense," Kate said, and put the telephone down.

"That was Mr Yallett," she said. "He's coming to Rome. This weekend. I don't know why."

"So?"

"So I thought you should know."

"He was my brief, that's all. Over. What they call a purely professional relationship."

"That's how it should be of course," she said, admiring the audible quotation marks he had put around the last phrase. "I'm not so sure that's how he sees it."

The telephone rang again.

"If that's Mr Yallett, tell him to fuck off. Or don't answer."

But Kate had never acquired the indifference which would allow her to leave a ringing telephone unanswered as Belinda often did.

"Kate? I'm not interrupting, am I?"

"Oh it's you."

"Were you expecting someone else? You sound disappointed," Belinda said.

"Not disappointed. I was getting ready to bite his head off, that's all."

"Are you all right?"

"Fine, we're having a cup of tea."

"Oh good, then I haven't interrupted. It's just that you didn't sound all right when you answered. You sounded stressed. Mustn't get stressed, you know."

Kate laughed, "Easier for you, that, than for me, as we've often agreed."

"Listen, it's such a lovely day, going to be hot, I thought a picnic. On the Palatine. I'll see to the food. Livia's house, about half-past one. You'll have finished work by then, won't you?"

"It's a long way from Parioli. But why not? We'll be there."

"Where'll we be?" Gary said.

"A picnic lunch."

"Kids' stuff."

"Oh I don't know. You might even enjoy it."

XVII

Approaching Stephen's apartment, across the river in Piazza Piscinulla, on what Belinda thought of as the wrong side of Viale Trastevere, Erik stopped.

"Let's have a coffee."

In the bar he said, "I'll wait for you here. Honest, I can't face it. He'll make a scene. I know his scenes. It'll be easier all round if you go yourself."

There was a dewiness under his eyes.

"Please ...," he said, "I really can't, you must know I can't."

"Oh all right then," she said. "But it may take some time."

"It'll be better this way, believe me it really will."

She leaned over and kissed him

You really are a coward, she thought.

"Poor Stephen," she said.

"You won't tell him I'm down here, will you? You won't tell him anything yet. Promise."

"He'll have to know sometime," she said, not knowing herself what there was to know, not really.

Stephen answered the intercom more quickly than she had expected. The apartment door was open when she reached the landing. He looked terrible. He had several days' growth of grey grizzly beard and he was dressed in an old brown woollen gown. His feet were bare and very dirty. When she kissed him, his breath stank of stale liquor and days without toothpaste.

"You're the only person I could bear to ..."

"Not Erik?"

"Oh God, that was a mistake. I see that now. Oh yes, I was crazy about him but now I never want to see him again. Oh it's such hell. Why do we do it?"

There was more in that vein, there always is, while she busied herself setting out what she had brought him: *aranciata*, mineral water, Redoxon.

"You could probably do with an injection," she said, "but I'm not competent to give it. Needles, you know. Why didn't you call Sol, he's your sponsor."

"Oh, I couldn't, I've let him down."

"But that's what he's there for. He'd tell you that himself."

"I've been thinking seriously about killing myself. Then I thought, I won't give Erik that satisfaction, he's not worth it, little tart."

"Can't think it would please him, he'd be cut up, rather. Come let's get you settled."

The bed was filthy and there was a bucket with slimy vomit beside it. There was vomit on the sheets too. The smell in the bedroom was horrible. She got him into the chair and opened the window as wide as it could go.

"Just sit there while I clear this up. Where do you keep your sheets?"

"Why are you so good to me?"

"All part of the service, you'd do the same for me."

He got to his feet and stood, shaking, clutching the back of the chair to stop himself from falling.

"I feel suddenly much worse."

"Are you going to be sick again?"

Long pause. Then, "No, maybe not."

"Tell you what, I'll run you a bath. You'll feel better when you've had a bath."

She had to help him through, hold him steady while he climbed into the bath. Then she went back to the bedroom, looked out a clean towel and pyjamas, resumed her tidying. There were photographs among the bedclothes and some fallen to the floor. She collected them and set them on the bedside table. They were of school groups and boys and youths in games clothes or swimsuits. They couldn't be called pornographic, not exactly. Not even indecent, yet there was indecency in the thought of Stephen leafing through them in misery and indulging in sad fantasies. There was one of Erik lying on a bed, propped up on an elbow, and smoking a cigarette. The lower half of his body was hidden, the upper naked. She was tempted, momentarily, to keep it, for when he left her too. Most of the boys in the photographs were blond and looked English or German or North American.

Poor Stephen, she thought again, imagining him imagining these boys as he lay sick and in fear. You were always afraid when you were coming out of a succession of heavy sessions. She knew that, though her own drinking had taken a different form. The depression and terror were the same.

She took the dressing-gown Stephen had discarded through to the kitchen and put it in the washing-machine; it felt as if she was expunging disgrace. Then she found a tin of soup – Baxter's Beef Consommé from that delicatessen in Via Mario de' Fiori, opened it and put it to heat over a low flame. She looked at her watch; ten minutes to twelve.

He called from the bath. She told him to wait a moment, returned to the bedroom, put clean sheets on the bed, fetched the towel, helped him out of the bath, dried him, got him into pyjamas and back to bed. Then she fetched the soup, tested the temperature, and put one arm round Stephen while she held the mug to his lips and let him sip. He got perhaps a third down before he said 'that's enough' and sank back on the pillows. In a little she got him to swallow a couple of vitamin pills and the rest of the soup.

She put a glass of *aranciata* and a glass of mineral water on the table.

"Oh God," he said, and began to weep.

She stroked his hair.

"It's all right," she said, "we've all been where you are."

"Voices," he said. "I've had the voices, saying horrible things."

"They do," she said; "that's what they do, but you know they're not real. They're not out there. Other horrors?"

"No, just the voices. Erik's among them. Horrible, vile."

She mopped his brow with the clean towel.

"Poor you. You need to sleep."

"I'm afraid," he said. "I try to pray, but there are no words."

"I'm going to give you a couple of Mogadon," she said. "They'll let you sleep properly. Don't worry. I won't go till you're sound. And I'll be back. Don't worry, it'll be all right."

"Bless you. Why are you so good to me? I don't deserve it. I don't really hate Erik, but we're no good, not for each other, I knew that from the ..."

Belinda knew that Stephen kept a set of spare keys in a kitchen drawer. She took them with her. It was only as she descended the stairs that she remembered Erik would have a set of keys himself.

He was sitting at a table outside the bar. He looked up from his book. "OK?"

"Not precisely. Could be worse."

He stretched out a hand for hers.

"I really couldn't face it."

"No," she said, "I quite see that now."

72

XVIII

When Tom Durward came to Rome to write a novel a couple of years after Cambridge, there was a young prostitute he used to see on the Via Veneto. She was a flower in first bloom. It astonished him that she hadn't been plucked. That was his first, romantic thought; nonsense of course. But she was beautiful, lovely, with red-gold hair cut short and long gorgeous legs. She wore a dull gold dress brief as a legionary's tunic. He couldn't take his eyes off her. He returned to the street the next afternoon at the same hour. She smiled to him; it was almost, he thought, a shy smile. Her skin glowed. He approached her.

His experience was limited. Certainly he had never paid for sex. He had had a girlfriend at Cambridge from the autumn term of his second year. They went to bed after a first-night party at the ADC theatre. She had played Beatrice in that production, in which Tom had had the very minor role of Borachio. Actually she had had eyes only for Benedick, but, alas, Benedick was in love with Claudio. She was resigned to his unavailability, so took up with Tom. Her inexperience was equal to his. Their first fumblings were uncertain, but in time they arrived at an accommodation. Tom could still feel grateful for the confidence she had given him. She was called Caroline, as so many girls were then. Now he could picture her sturdy hockey-formed legs, but not her face. Her stage career hadn't – surely? – survived Cambridge, unlike Benedick's. Benedick indeed was now a knight, Sir Llewellyn Rhys-Davies – how assiduously he had polished his Welsh accent away, just before regional accents became the fashion.

Durward sat drinking coffee on the terrace of the Café de Paris, and looked down the tree-lined street, past the news-stand, to the corner where the girl Elsa had had her stance, with one knee bent and her gold-sandalled foot resting against the wall. They had gone to a dingy hotel in one of the little streets between the Veneto and Trinità dei Monti. It probably didn't survive now, not as it had been then.

That was a few years before he had a connection with the film industry, which was a pity, because it was naturally the girl's ambition to get into movies, and naively, touchingly indeed, she had chosen that stance in the hope of being "spotted" by a producer or agent. They had gone together a few times, though Tom couldn't afford her, just as he couldn't afford usually to eat and drink at the bars on the Via Veneto, where a chicken sandwich cost more than a dinner with pasta and meat in the sort of trattoria he was accustomed to. But he did so occasionally when he had come to collect mail from Thomas Cook's, because it seemed the thing to do, just as when visiting London from Cambridge he and his friends would gravitate to the American Bar of the Ritz or Jules in Jermyn Street.

Perhaps because, being young, he made an agreeable change from her usual clients, she even went with him a few times when he wasn't in funds, not certainly to the hotel, which was after all for her a place of work, but to stroll in the Borghese Gardens. They held hands as if they were real lovers.

He never found her more desirable than when they were walking the dusty paths with their little fingers crooked together. She talked freely, between long happy silences, but his Italian was poor, and in any case she had a strong accent, Roman or of some other region he couldn't tell, and he understood no more than a third of what she said.

Then one day – and the next and the next – she was gone from the street, and he never saw her again. But for a long time, after calling at Cook's, he would drink coffee or a whisky at the Café de Paris, and keep his eyes fixed on the spot where she had stood. He would then walk up the hill and into the gardens to a certain fountain, its stone discoloured by weather and old moss, where one day she had perched on the rim allowing him to take photographs. There was one he had kept in his wallet for years. It showed her with her head lowered so that her face was in shadow, and she was looking at him sideways, while the fingers of her right hand rested on the hem of her short skirt, which was rucked up just a little to reveal a long line of lovely thigh.

The photograph had long disappeared, but he didn't need it really; it was in his mind's eye. And it was on its account that he now turned up the hill towards the gardens in search of the fountain and his lost youth.

She had had a black eye, discoloured anyway, that day, powdered to conceal the bruise; and that was doubtless why she had held her head at that angle which, even now almost forty years on he recalled with longing, part lust, part regret.

So it was necessary to find the fountain and there recapture also the moment when, descending, she had stumbled, gone over her ankle, and swayed off-balance into his arms. Then she had turned her face to his and let him kiss her, first, tenderly, no more than a brush of the lips, on the bruised eye, and then on her mouth.

What was it they said then? Could he hear its echo now in the gently plashing water? And did it matter?

He stretched out his hands, cupped them, and drank. What had become of her?

Chapter Eighteen

The separateness of lives once joined appalled him, like the sun dipping behind a black cloud and leaving him to shiver in the shade of pinetrees. That morning he had telephoned Meg Baillie and arranged to meet her at Rosati, and then lunch. Now he wished he hadn't. If his memories of Elsa belonged to the young, eager and, in some respects at least, admirable Tom Durward, Meg had risen a ghostly figure from years the memory of which filled him with shame. She was, evidently, one of those he had wronged – one of so many, and yet she seemed happy to meet him again. It was after all she who had addressed him the other evening, and he had heard welcome in her telephone voice a couple of hours ago.

"I hear you were a great success last night," she said.

He bridled, like a schoolboy embarrassed to be singled out for public praise. Yet he couldn't resist asking who she had heard it from.

"The Marchesa," she said.

"Marchesa?"

"Belinda, I call her the Marchesa because it puts her at a distance, and she really is a Marchesa as a result of her last marriage. I'm fond of her but a little in awe too, she's so self-sufficient. Anyway you impressed her. Yes, let's do, have lunch, I mean ..."

The last words came in a rush as if her irony at the expense of Belinda might have caused him to withdraw his invitation.

Things do transpire about people. Who had said that? Good word, transpire, anyway. Someone about Conrad, he thought. Greene? Fitzgerald?

Cigar in the corner of his mouth, and leaning, sometimes heavily, on his stick, Tom limped along the Via del Babuino, past the English church, dating from the days when the area around Piazza di Spagna was known as the *ghetto inglese*.

She wasn't alone. He had sandy hair, a sandy scrub of beard, and a face that expressed resentment, perhaps defiance. He and Meg weren't talking, but had the air of being enclosed in a silence that was part of a long angry dialogue. As Tom waited to cross the street, he thought it might be better – more tactful – to turn away, but she looked up, saw him, raised her hand, and denied him the choice.

"As you can see, Mike's turned up."

"What my wife means," Mike said, "is that to her dismay I've crashed your party. Sorry." He picked up his glass of beer and drank half in one swallow. "I'll bugger off of course if you insist."

"Why should I do that?"

In the restaurant Mike called for a litre of white wine.

"Half a litre," Meg said.

"A litre." Mike held the waiter's sleeve to make sure his order was taken. "Meg tells me you were the sensation of the meeting last night. As you can see I'm off the wagon. Does that worry you?"

"You're making a mistake, but you know that, and it's your life."

"Mine too," Meg said.

"But for how much longer? My wife's my severest critic. Who wants that? Who can live with a critic? She says my new novel's crap."

"It's not new," Meg said, "it's recycled. He won't write, can't write about anything but himself and booze. Crap's putting it mildly."

"You see. She's written me off. So has Kate. She's my sponsor, or supposed to be but she's ditched me for a pretty boy murderer."

"You haven't seen him. You don't know he's pretty. You don't even know he's a murderer."

"Of course he's a murderer, Kate wouldn't be interested otherwise. And of course he's pretty. Where the hell's that wine?"

"I've met him," Tom said. "I wouldn't call him pretty."

"Oh, you're a man of the world, are you? You know things ... But this time you're wrong. Stands to reason he's pretty. Why would Kate be interested otherwise? She's that age."

"You're confusing her with Belinda," Meg said. "Anyway her Dutch Nazi wasn't pretty, was he?"

"Belgian," Mike said. "You see, my wife gets everything wrong."

The waiter brought wine and food, ravioli for Mike, *spaghetti alle vongole* for the other two. Mike seized the carafe, poured himself a glass, downed it, then poured another and one for Meg.

"Go on," he said, "drink it. My wife drinks like a fish, but she has no drinking problem. No problem with alcohol, none at all. Just like my late by me unlamented brother-in-law. Never sober, queer as they come, but he had no drinking problem, that's official, the official line."

"I knew Eddie," Tom said. "I liked him a lot. He wasn't queer."

"Is that so? Doesn't matter, he was no good, Eddie, no good at all. Between you and me, a little rat. My wife doesn't like me to say these things."

"Oh shut up, Mike, for Christ's sake, eat your ravioli and shut up." She was near to tears. "I'm sorry," she said to Tom. "I didn't mean it to be like this. See if you can ... I can't stand it, sorry."

She got up and blundering to the door left them.

78

Tom, wondering if he should have followed, forked his spaghetti.

"We all go into the dark," Mike said. "Spoiled your date, haven't I?"

"I wouldn't call it a date. As she said, you should eat."

XIX

"You can't blame him," Belinda said.

"But I don't, believe me."

"I mean, to be thrown among people who look at you as if you were an animal in the zoo. I can quite see why he needs to be on his own. Not that he isn't on his own when he's with us. He is, isn't he?"

Kate nibbled at a stem of sun-burned grass.

They were lying in the shade of the pines. The hill was deserted, except for a German couple on a bench a little way off, engaged in possibly intellectual argument. Gary was leaning on the railing that surmounted the wall and looking out over the valley in which lay the Circus Maximus. Erik slept, stretched on his belly, his head resting on his folded arms. Three o'clock, the quiet hour of the day, even the traffic from the Via dei Fori Imperiali no more than a hum, less obtrusive than the rattle of the cicadas.

"How do you feel about him?" Belinda said. "Do you like him?"

"Like? That's not the point. I haven't yet penetrated the shell."

"You don't feel ... repugnance?"

"You do?"

"I thought I would. I got Kenneth, you know, to fax me accounts of the murder and the trial. It was pretty horrible, wasn't it?"

"Indeed yes," Kate said. "I wouldn't deny that for a moment. I'm never convinced though that people are what they do."

"So you think now he was guilty?"

"Oh yes, I've never really had any doubt, whatever I said. Nor does his mother. I could see that. But so what? Doesn't stop her loving him, being ready to fight anyone for him, lie for him of course till she's blue in the face. And quite right too in my opinion. She's a good woman. And you Bel, expected to feel repugnance, but you don't really, do you?"

"He's just a boy, isn't he? Not that that means anything either way. What are you really looking for, Kate?"

"I like knowing about people. It's my sort of exploration."

"Why he did it, you mean?"

"Not really. I never think why answers anything. Why did we drink? Why are we alcoholic when others who drank more aren't? Why do you fancy Erik, if it comes to that? You do, don't you?

"Oh sort of," she said, "but that's sex. Different. You don't find Gary sexy?"

"I can see that he could be. But no, I don't. He's a bit pathetic, and yet he's not at all pathetic. That's interesting."

Belinda lit a cigarette, and watched the smoke curl deep-grey against the deeper blue of a sky which was touched with gold only at the edges.

"What a pair we are," she said. "What would anyone looking at our picnic party think?"

"What indeed?"

"Two old bags and their toy-boys, that's what. Or don't they say toy-boys now? Is that last year's word? Is Gary gay? Do you think he is?"

"Does Erik? He should know."

"Oh Erik's afraid of him. He tries to hide it, but he's afraid. Fascinated too, but afraid. I see what you mean though about the little cough. It's rather sweet, even endearing. And he has good manners, though he tries to act as if he hadn't."

"You noticed that too," Kate said. "He's a mother's boy really. But gay? I think not. He's a

Puritan, a very English Puritan. I can always spot it, it's the Latin in me. Hates the flesh. Have you watched him eat?"

"Yes. He nibbles."

"Like it's an unpleasant duty. He told me off for smoking too much this morning."

They strolled through the trees, skirting the fenced-off bits of ground where excavations of the imperial palaces were being conducted at a pace so slow you might think eternity would not suffice to reveal all there had been of the Eternal City – a line Belinda had heard from Mike Baillie, but assumed (correctly) did not originate with him.

Kate put her hand on Belinda's arm.

"Reynard's coming out this weekend."

"And that worries you?"

"Yes. Yes, it does. I don't understand why he's coming. Barristers don't usually pursue their ex-clients, do they?"

"Not at all. It's even against the rules, I think. In any case it's the solicitor, isn't it, who's the client, not the accused? Reynard made a good job of the trial though, didn't he? That was the impression from reading the faxes. But, if you want my opinion, the answer in one word is mischief ..."

"He makes Gary nervous."

"He makes me nervous. Or used to. I nearly married him once, remember. I was crazy about him until, well, it evaporated."

"Would you mind meeting him again?"

They leaned on the rail and looked out over the Forum.

"There's something of the Roman Emperor in Reynard," Belinda said. "One of the mad ones."

"I've always been surprised he goes in for defending."

"Oh no, defending poor brutes gives him a kick. It's not kindness or generosity, you know. They're so dependent on him, at his mercy. Mind you he did once say that if we still hanged people he would have liked to be a judge. He wasn't joking. That was when I began to go off him. Who was the judge who had to change his knickers after pronouncing the death sentence?"

"Said to be Goddard, but I doubt the story. I mean, who would know?"

"His clerk?"

"But would he tell?"

"Why not?" Belinda said. "It's only in sentimental novels servants are loyal. Think how telling would go down in the Saloon Bar."

"You may be right. I see of course that defending can appeal to the sadist. And Reynard is one, isn't he? People who've never tried have no notion how satisfying being nasty can be. I noticed that a long time ago. Actually, I've got a rather nasty experiment in mind myself."

XX

"I guess that's the most horrible place I've been in," Erik said. "It was kind of gruesome."

Belinda didn't immediately reply. They were sitting outside a bar by the Teatro Marcello. Kate and Gary had taken the bus back to Parioli.

"You know, I could get to like Gary," Erik said. "I never thought I would hear myself say that. But I could get to like him if he'd let me. He won't though. He won't open up. It's like ... I don't know what it's like – something I can't express. Did you see when Kate put her hand on his shoulder?"

"Yes, I saw."

"It was like it frightened him." He sipped his Coca-Cola. "Why d'you think she was so keen to take us there? It was her idea, wasn't it, not yours."

"Yes, it was her idea."

"That's a relief. Really. I wouldn't have known what to think if you'd said it was your idea. Was it a kind of test, for Gary? A tad nasty?"

Belinda couldn't answer that one, not out loud and not even really in her own mind. "Oh I don't know," she said.

"I'm not sorry I've seen it," Erik said, "the way you are not sorry you've seen a horror movie even if it scared you shitless. I've read about the Mamertine, in the guidebooks and in a novel about Tiberius. That's how I knew about Sejanus. The guy who wrote the novel got it wrong though. He said Sejanus was thrust down that twisting stair. But the stair wasn't constructed till the Middle Ages. Before then they dropped the prisoners through a hole in the roof, and I guess the executioners descended the same way. Sejanus was strangled you know. Do you think it's true Jugurtha was stripped naked before they threw him in and that he chewed his own arm because he was starving? That's what the story says."

"There's no story so horrible it can't be true," Belinda said. "Surely we know that now." Erik flicked a lighter towards Belinda's cigarette. He took a spoonful of ice cream and just touched it with his tongue.

"What do you think Kate hoped to learn about Gary from taking us there?"

Belinda looked away. Erik put the spoon in his mouth, holding it there while he allowed the ice cream to begin to melt.

"I guess that place is evil," he said. "You get the feeling it is, don't you. Emanation – that's the word, emanations of evil. Do you think she wanted to test his response to that? Or is that kind of fanciful?"

Again Belinda didn't reply. She looked out through the smoke rising from her cigarette to the rocks of the Capitol across the road down which the traffic streamed.

"I'm nervous," Erik said. "That's why I'm talking too much. He didn't show anything, did he, not till she put her hand on his shoulder and he shook it off. With a sort of shudder like."

Belinda thought: it was Reynard took me there, my only previous visit. It excited him too. It excited him no end. It was there he asked me to marry him, in the execution chamber. Would you believe it? I would have refused him anyway, but ... that made it easy. I don't think I've ever told Kate that, no reason to; I don't think I've ever said outright more than I said this afternoon, that I nearly married him once. Would it excite Erik now, if I told him I had a proposal of marriage there? I hope not, but ...

"Does Kate think Gary's in love with death?"

Chapter Twenty

"Is anyone really?"

"Necrophilia's not just dead bodies," Erik said. "I've read somewhere, that it's not always sexual. Maybe Edgar Allan Poe. What do you think?"

Belinda had two thoughts which she couldn't speak: first that Erik himself was too excited by the Mamertine, and second that she would like to know what he expected from ... what? ... life? ... her? But she couldn't speak the criticism, and as for the question – she feared his answer. She didn't care to take the risk.

XXI

Leg was hurting. Not for the first time Tom wondered if a doctor would recommend a hip replacement. He leaned heavily on his stick. No doctor would get the chance. He'd walked too far, that was all. But the Via Giulia at twilight, the warm facades of the lovely buildings in deepening, almost purple shadow, worth an ache in hip and leg to limp its length.

It was again the bad time of day. It's worse in Rome than in any other city I know, he thought, except Venice of course, and the natural thing is to go and have a drink that will dull the solitude that is so sharp in the half-light. But you can't do that and, touch wood, you don't even want to. You ought to be glad of that, but it's like when you've broken with a woman and there is that emptiness ...

A man who might have been old, sitting with his back to the wall of a house that was some kind of government building according to the plaque by the door, extended an open hand in his direction. There was a bottle between the man's legs, and a big shaggy dog slept by him with one eye half open. Tom nodded and fished a note from his breast pocket and pushed it at the man. Often in his drinking years he'd pictured himself in the man's position.

He should have gone after Meg when she ran out of the restaurant. If he'd done so, they might be in bed now. Or not; it would be grotesque if they had really done that so many years back. With his belly and his hip and now his impotence, it didn't bear thinking on.

Mike was in a mess, a sad mess. He ought to feel for him, as with the beggar and his dog. But the beggar asked only for money, or could be forgotten after money changed hands. Mike demanded what Durward was in no mood, or even condition, to give.

In Piazza Farnese a boy with tangled curls smiled at him. The boy was sitting sideways on his scooter with one knee pulled up against his chest. He asked for a cigarette. Tom shook a couple from his packet of untipped Camels, and lit one. The boy looked over the flame and the eyes and smile and posture told Tom he was available.

"Nothing doing," Tom said in Italian, "you've got the wrong guy."

"Hey, I didn't really think you were queer," the boy said. "I was just passing the time. I'm waiting for my girl."

"Lucky you. Congratulations."

"And I deserve them, she's quite something."

"The best ones always keep you waiting," Tom said. "Have patience and then enjoy yourself."

Turning into Campo de' Fiori he settled at a table outside a bar on the river side of the square. The blonde woman greeted him as one who had established himself as a regular, and fetched him an espresso and a half-litre of mineral water. It pleased him to be accepted this way; he had always liked to form a routine for himself.

He thought about the boy on the scooter and how it might have been if he had been that way. You couldn't – he drew on his *toscano* – pretend you have been a happy success with women. There's only so much that even the best or worst of them can take. But the other, no, not at all. He'd been afraid for Jamie when he sent him to Stowe because Jamie was blond and brave and ingenuous. And then he was dead, drowned in that beautiful, level, loathly lake. They called it an accident. Tom tried to persuade himself it was.

For a long time subsequently he played the Hemingway man, destroyed but not defeated. He read Hemingway and cried over the good sentences. "In the Fall the war was always there, but we did not go to it any more ..." But it was the old Colonel in *Across the River and into the Trees* that he made himself into. Those who knew about such matters and set up as critics panned that novel. One, Tom remembered, dismissed the old lion as a "garrulous buffoon" because he was capable of proclaiming *Across* his best work. Well, he hadn't been there, that critic. Tom had. Sure it wasn't his best work – that was to be found in the short stories, a few pages of *To Have And Have Not* and the bits of *A Moveable Feast* where there were no other writers present. But Tom would rather have written *Across* than, hell, have got tenure as a Distinguished Professor. The duck-shooting on the lagoon made the spine tingle, no matter how often you read it.

Well, it was years since Tom had been the Colonel, but Hem and the Colonel had seen him into and through bad times.

You could make a wonderful mood movie of *Across*. He'd written it himself, keeping at most five per cent of the dialogue which was mostly so corny and embarrassing. Lew Silcouth was interested, enthusiastic, keen to produce it, then went off his head, choked to death on his own vomit. So there it was, or rather wasn't. Tom had no copy even of his screenplay.

A flock of starlings wheeled like acrobats across the darkening sky. Tom called for another espresso, and he saw Belinda and the soft boy Erik come into the piazza. They approached his table, exchanged greetings, settled there.

"You haven't seen Stephen, have you?" Belinda said.

Chapter Twenty-One

"Stephen?"

"Stephen Mallany. You remember, you said he was like a Church of England vicar."

"Oh him, I didn't know that was his name."

"He's gone missing again," Belinda said. "He's drinking, we're sure of that. So we've been searching …"

"It's hopeless," Erik said. "I mean, we've no idea, just none. We've hunted all over Trastevere." He flashed a smile at Tom. "Bel's exhausted." He sought to draw Tom into complicity.

"Just anxious," she said.

"Mallany," Tom said.

He lifted his hand. The blonde woman came and took their order: Schweppes Tonic for Belinda, Diet Coke for the boy. She looked like a tougher younger version of Belinda; not fresher; she'd been through it herself, and it showed.

Erik said, "I'm glad we've met, wanted to tell you how good I thought your story was, really helpful. I was too shy, I guess, to say more than thank you yesterday."

The words came in a rush, but prepared and stored up.

"These starlings are quite something," Tom said, "just look at them. Mallany."

"You sound as if it means something to you."

"It does, indeed it does."

"I'm sure you could help Stephen," Erik said. "When we find him that is. I think he'd listen to you. I can't say anything to him, and I'm not sure Bel can either, can you?"

"He's in full flight," Belinda said.

"I hate this side of AA," Tom said. "It embarrasses me. Never been happy with the Good Samaritan."

"Flight's the wrong word," Belinda said. She sipped her Schweppes, "Stephen used to fly very prettily when I first knew him, and he was sweet then, but now ... his wings are damaged."

"This isn't a good city for a bender," Tom said. "It frightens the Italians."

"Why's that?" Erik said.

"Drunks make them nervous."

"Stephen's not a violent drunk," Erik said. "Least, I've never seen him ... he's never hit anyone, I'm sure. He starts crying."

"Oh yes," Tom said, "we're all screaming like abused and abandoned children.

"You don't believe that," Belinda said.

"Believe that shaming purple prose? Let's call it ironical. We're all into irony now. It's the only defence left us."

"Defence against what?" Erik said.

"Take your pick. Reality? Sincerity? Truth?"

XXII

Rain in the night had washed the dust from the oleander leaves. Now, seven in the morning, Parioli sparkled. There was more of autumn in the air. Kate stood on the balcony and breathed deeply – in, out, in, out, twenty times – before she allowed herself the first cigarette of the day.

Then she took a pot of coffee to her writing-desk and began to transcribe her tapes. She wrote up the account of the visit to the Mamertine; that had gone well. When she placed her hand on Gary's shoulder, she felt his tension. On the way home they stopped outside a cutler's. Gary examined the knives in the window. She asked if he wanted one. He looked her in the face, then his eyes slid away, and he lowered his head and mumbled words she didn't catch. In the evening he announced he was going for a walk and looked
at her as if he expected she would either insist on accompanying him or try to stop him. But she said nothing. He returned an hour later, and said, "Mr Yallett's coming just for the weekend, that's right, isn't it?" Then, "Why's he coming? Are you two up to something?"

"I didn't invite him," Kate said.

Now she wrote: he doesn't like being put in a position where he has to ask questions. Evidence of a deficiency in self-confidence? Is that why he feels always under threat? He's disconcerted, even alarmed, by the prospect of Yallett's visit.

She drank a cup of coffee; wrote, "In *The Politics of the Family*, R. D. Laing says that he considers many adults, among whom he includes himself, to exist in a species of hypnotic trance, induced in early infancy; we remain, he thinks, in this state unless – 'when we dead awaken,' as Ibsen has it – unless that happens, it's as if we have never lived."

"He was such a happy child, as a kid," his mother said to me. "Then his father went away and he took charge of me. That was till he was twelve or thirteen, and he got in with a bad lot, easy to do that round here."

So the hypnotic trance came later than infancy in this case. But species of hypnotic trance – yes. Laing was only half a charlatan, the other half genius. Would he have got through to someone as carapaced as Gary, who shrinks from physical contact which Laing valued so highly? A knife keeps all bodies at a distance, unless or until …

The telephone rang.

"Meg here, sorry to interrupt you, Kate, but have you seen him? He's not with you, is he?"

"No. He's still at it then. I thought he was winding down?"

"Some hope. Christ knows where he is. I rather think I've had enough, all I can take. I know it's early in the day for such decisions, but then I haven't slept all night. He wasn't pleased, you know, when you said you'd have no time for him for the next while. She is my bloody sponsor, he kept saying. Not that I'm blaming you, Kate. I'm not even blaming myself. I'm too busy breathing fire in the old brute's direction. Or I was, till I said, to hell with him."

"But you still called me, Meg."

"Well, yes, you can't throw off responsibility as easily as you throw off love, can you?"

"Some people would put that the other way round."

"I guess they would. Oh hell."

"You could try Sol," Kate said. "Mike has a great respect for Sol. We all have of course."

Chapter Twenty-Two

"OK, but I suppose the old bugger'll turn up, when he's through. He always has."

It was eight o'clock. Yallett's plane got in at 10.30. She made a cup of tea and took it through to Gary's room. He was still asleep, lying on his belly, his face turned to the wall. He made a little grinding noise with his teeth. She opened the shutters to let the sunlight in. Falling on his cheek it turned the skin the colour of unsalted butter. She laid the cup on the table by the bed and left him to sleep. Reynard could make his own way from the airport. She had said she would meet him and was pleased not to. In sleep Gary looked easy, even happy. When she had asked him about bad dreams, he denied ever having them. She thought he might be speaking the truth there.

She returned to her notes and leafed back to read again his version of the night of the killing.

XXIII

Reynard Yallett waited less than five minutes at Arrivals before he called Kate, mobile to mobile.

"Are you on your way?"

"No," she said. "It wasn't possible. We'll meet you for lunch. Say 1.30 or a little later. Vecchia Roma, Piazza Campitelli. You'll find it with no difficulty."

She rang off. Yallett smiled. He liked the way she had offered no excuse; that was the real bitch. He liked the hostility in her voice. He strode out of the airport towards the taxi rank. There was a fast train service to Termini now, but it wasn't for him.

"Hotel Excelsior, Via Veneto."

The day sparkled. He felt good. He felt dangerous.

He savoured the thought of the interview he had given a girl journalist last night: for *The Sunday Times* Colour Magazine. "I despised my father," he told her, "and his limp post-Christian morality. They made him a bishop, you know, and all his philosophy was wet liberalism." Now he smiled to see again the skinny girl's eager greedy mouth. He'd leaned forward, and pressed the stop button on her recorder, and put his hands round her waist to draw her to her feet; and then he had forced open her linen trousers, colour of ripe peaches, and searched deeper, while she thrust her tongue into his mouth, and they staggered locked together to the bed where he took her quickly, with no words, and she moaned and cried out for more. That was his way and he had his father to thank. The contempt with which he'd spoken of him had excited her.

He had her three times, once up the arse, where she'd never had it before. She cried a little, and took a shower, and dressed, in tears again, because it was the first time, she said, she had cheated on her husband. She was twenty-seven and he didn't believe her.

"Come to Rome with me tomorrow."

She sat on the edge of the bed, her short ragged-cut dark hair and flat chest making her look like a ruined child, and shook her head, not looking at him.

"You never finished your interview."

"It's not possible," she said. "I just can't."

"All right," he said. "Tuesday, here, six o'clock."

"I don't know."

"You do, really. Six o'clock. You'll come."

He reached up and pulled her over him, and let his hand fall smart on her buttocks. He held her like that several minutes.

Now he held the memory, rolled it around. What had she said to her husband when she got home? "Oh yes, sure, it went well, but we got interrupted, so I have to go back on Tuesday to finish it, rather a nuisance, darling, on account of my deadline." And the husband would say, "Is he the monster he's painted as, the genuine Rottweiler?" And she would smile – a smile to conceal her excitement – the knowledge that he, Reynard, knew her better than she had known herself till that afternoon ... Oh yes, he could imagine the scene, just as surely as he could still smell her skin on his, such a slut beneath that glossy Soho House exterior.

They had arrived in the Via Veneto and he had seen nothing of the drive into Rome.

There were faxes awaiting him at the hotel desk. There always were. There would be e-mails too. Reynard Yallett was ever in demand. He impressed himself on the desk clerk. He exuded authority. At seventeen a rebel, a problem provoking long discussions – "What shall we do with Reynard? What can we make of him?" – now, at forty-five, Reynard Yallett knew himself to be formidable, and feared. And "they" had nothing to do with it. He was a self-created man. It gave him a kick to know he was disliked. Let them hate, provided they fear.

And now this weekend promised amusement. Kate Sturzo was formidable too, in her own way, steel there. Her preoccupation with evil wasn't just academic.

And the Chicken. The Chicken had held his interest from their first interview, when they had sat for fully five minutes, eyes fixed on each other, before the Chicken submitted and looked away. His confederates were ordinary scum, the sweepings of South London. But there was something to the Chicken, a boy whose life had been passed east of Eden.

He looked the Chicken over: the smooth, never shaven cheek, the old eyes under the soft hair. There was a touch of colour to him now, a buttery sheen imparted by autumn sun. They sat – it was just warm enough – at a table outside the restaurant. Saturday lunch, most tables were occupied in the little enclosure, protected from the street by a child-sized fence through which and around which grew a dark green dusty hedge. Reynard took it in: Italians mostly, except for one table of obvious Americans, and another small one at which two young people, Americans also, sat opposite each other, silent, the boy studying a street-map, the girl reading a paperback. She was blonde, puppy-fat gleaming on her brown naked legs.

He talked to Kate, stories of the courts, the BBC, some politicians, common acquaintances. He drank wine, hesitating as he lifted the glass, to taunt the others for not joining him.

Chapter Twenty-Three

"Don't you miss it? You were such a sparkler in your drinking days."

"Oh, I was, wasn't I," Kate said, "a sparkler."

Gary crumbled his bread, ate little. His fingers were long, thin, the nails bitten to the quick.

Reynard said, "One of these French novelists – you'll remember which, I'm sure – has one of his characters, a spoiled intellectual, naturally, commit a murder just to see what it feels like. He's nothing against the victim, you understand. It's just an *acte gratuit* – that was the phrase, wasn't it? The idea seemed outlandish, shocking in 1900 or whenever it was. It's commonplace now, happens all the time. Just this week – you'll read about it when our rickety legal machine creaks into action – I was brought such a case. Four boys, about Gary's age, two of them, but the youngest only fourteen, stopped a young man just after midnight up Ladbroke Grove way. Nice young man, so they roughed him up, just a little at first, for fun, then tied him up, shoved him in the back of a stolen car – and what they said made him piss himself. They stopped on the bank of the canal, got out, leaving him there, and pushed the car into the water.

"Some old biddy saw it, called the police who, amazingly, responded, and they found the four of them sitting by the canal drinking vodka, smoking dope, and giggling. There's not much of a defence."

XXIV

"Sorry, I can't eat any more," Meg said, "It's the first real meal I've had in days."

"That's all right," Tom said. "You know, drunks look after themselves, somehow, usually. He's probably holed up in a hotel."

"Is that what you used to do?"

"It is indeed. You can feel safe in hotels. Nobody who cares can get at you. Of course sometimes there's nobody that does care."

Meg lit a cigarette, and looked beyond him, across the piazza, to the Pantheon and the never-ending flow of tourists.

"He says, you know, that if the writing came right again, then he wouldn't need to drink, not the way he does, as an alcoholic. He could be a normal social drinker again. That's what he says."

"We've all said that or something like it. If only ... How did he drink when you first knew him?"

She paused, tipped the ash off her cigarette, screwed up her face, picked up her dark glasses, but didn't put them on.

"I want to get this right, I'd like to be fair. Heavy, yes, very heavy, but most of us were that then, weren't we? There was nothing he liked better than holding court, in a bar or over a restaurant table. He was good fun, I have to remember that. And later when he was dry – and he's been dry for long periods, months sometimes, it was different. He started saying he couldn't stand other people without a drink. He couldn't stand me either."

"Read one of his novels once," Tom said. "May have been his first, about a group of undergraduates following the bulls. Fake mostly, ersatz Hemingway, but there was something there. The dialogue was lively as I recall."

"It won prizes that book. But Mike knows how much was fake. Then he wrote a couple that were sincere, one about middle-class life in Glasgow, and good really, the critics weren't interested and sales were awful. His publishers lost interest too. That was four, five years ago. So I feel sorry for him and he can't stand that. I can't stand it myself. Nothing kills a relationship more surely than one partner feeling sorry for the other. That's how it seems to me."

Tom lifted a hand to call the waiter to them and ordered coffee.

"Would you like a grappa?" he said. "Or something. I don't mind, really. It doesn't disturb me."

"Did it once?"

"Sure it did."

"I don't think I will," she said, "but thank you."

"Just coffee then," Tom said. "*Due espressi.*"

"If he wasn't so bad," Meg said, "I could leave him. I did, actually. Last summer. We were in Spain. He'd been commissioned by a Sunday paper to write a piece for their colour magazine – he can still do that sort of thing. It was about, I can't remember his name, the young Englishman who's set out to be a bullfighter – this on the strength of that novel written more than a dozen years ago. Which struck me as pathetic. We were in Salamanca. I was sitting by the window of our hotel room looking at the storks standing by their big ragged nest on a church tower across the way. I liked the storks, they could do nothing for such a long time, bit like Belinda really. It was kind of peaceful. Mike was tapping away on his typewriter. Then he gave me his article to read, which he almost never does. He was smiling the wrong sort of smile. I said it was cheap, what he'd written. 'They pay well,' he said. 'It's still cheap,' I said. 'You won't object to spending the money,' he said, and hit me, quite hard, hard enough

100

to knock me off the chair. Then he went off. I knew he was heading for a bar. He'd never hit me before, never got beyond clenching his fists. That was when I decided to get out. I packed my bag. Before I left the room I looked out of the window. The storks were still there in just the same attitudes. They hadn't moved. There'd been this sordid little domestic drama and the storks hadn't moved. I had to wait hours at the station, there aren't many trains to Madrid from Salamanca. I called him a couple of days later and he joined me. I felt guilty he'd written something so cheap. It makes no sense to me but that's how it was. He didn't apologise. We just carried on as if nothing had happened. But he's made no effort to control his drinking since, even if he still goes to AA. Or rather I got him to return and he went to get me off his back. Why am I telling you all this?"

Why was she? Because she had to tell someone? Because Eddie was dead and he was the closest to Eddie she had left, or at least to hand?

She said, "Could he be right? If he could write the way he thinks he is meant to write, could he stop drinking then?"

Tom Durward took his time. He cut a *toscano* in half and lit it.

"That's what he says?"

"Sometimes ... often."

"I wish it was true," he said, "but it's the booze that's the problem, not the writing."

She began to cry. He looked away, into the sunshine. She cried silently for perhaps two minutes. Then she got up and went through to the Ladies' room to recover and repair. What he hadn't said: I felt that way for years. But then, earlier, when I was young, I often thought: if I can write one book that is really good and true, it doesn't matter what sort of a mess I make of my life otherwise. Which was nonsense. Sadly. A book written was something consigned to the past, far more completely than the affairs of your non-writing life which stayed alive to delight or disturb or haunt or pain you. Whereas the written book was dead to its author. He had indeed brought off once, maybe twice, what he had aspired to do. And now, these books meant nothing to him. They had been thrown into the world, and, if they mattered at all, it was to other people that they mattered now.

"I'm sorry about that," Meg said, returning. "It's because what you said is what I know, only I've been trying to deny it, just as Mike does, and that's because it's easier to kid myself he might write well again than to believe he can stop drinking. Does that make sense?"

"Oh yes, only too good sense. But it's a waste of time to think of the 'whys'. The only question that matters is how you stop yourself taking that first drink. We have so many ways of persuading ourselves we're entitled to it, some more shameful than Mike's. You reminded me of that the other night, how I used what happened to Jamie ..."

"I was never clear about that," she said, "but I know it was terrible. Like Eddie for me, but I could see it coming to Eddie. He was on his way down already. Which was sad enough."

For a little they sat, not talking. Maybe both thinking about Eddie, and how lives go wrong. Eddie had challenged the gods, knocked the heads off the Hermes, and then, Tom didn't know but supposed, he woke one morning and was no longer young and the weather was cold and grey.

"Can we walk a bit?" Meg said.

"Sure, why not?"

"All right for you, with your leg?"

"Good for it."

A troop of tourists – Japanese, Americans, Germans, English too, he supposed – emerged from the Pantheon.

"What do they make of it, do you think?" Meg said. "No, that's silly and patronising. What do I make of it after all? Or you? You're not religious, are you?"

"I don't know. The Latin word, *religio*, originally meant just 'attention', paying heed to the things you must do. I might be religious in that sense, like Dr Johnson touching lamp posts."

Meg said, "I was brought up religious. So was Eddie. When he was twelve or thirteen he was going to be a priest."

Maybe he should have stuck to it. Tom kept the words to himself. He had a knack of making words come out bitter even when he hadn't thought them that way. Maybe Eddie should have stuck to it. He gestured towards the Pantheon again.

"Some pope, forget which, had twenty-eight wagon-loads of martyrs' bones brought from the catacombs and buried there, under the floor."

"Bit morbid," she said. "Of course I see the point of morbidity. Thinking about Mike encourages outbursts of it, if you can have an outburst of morbidity, I wouldn't know." They stopped to buy Meg an ice cream.

"How odd," she said, "to think of everyone who has walked these streets, with their problems, over the last couple of thousand years, and here we are. And you still see the same faces, from Renaissance paintings, a Raphael here, a Caravaggio there – look at that boy for instance. Is that true of anywhere else, do you think?"

Chapter Twenty-Four

"They'd more painters in Rome than elsewhere," Tom said.

They crossed the Corso, walked a bit up the noisy bustling Via del Tritone, till they were past the square with the post office and the buses, and then, turning left, made their way through narrow expensive streets to the Piazza di Spagna and mounted the steps towards Trinità dei Monti.

A dozen steps up Meg clutched Tom's arm.

"Oh no," she said, and led him over to the wall against the Keats-Shelley house. A man was lying there, a bottle of grappa, almost empty, by his right hand. His mouth was open and his eye was bruised and bleeding. He had lost one shoe, his shirt was unbuttoned, and the zip of his trousers undone.

"It's Stephen," she said. "Oh God."

"Stephen?"

"Stephen Mallany, he's a friend of Mike's, sort of. They were on this bender together ... If Mike did this to him ..."

Tom got one arm under him, a dead weight. He couldn't have been there long ... the police ... even now. Tom stopped a young man descending the steps, asked for help. Together they heaved him upright.

"Go down and get a taxi," Tom said. "Tell him we'll pay double fare, say there's been an accident."

XXV

They took him to Meg's apartment in Via Milano, and laid him on the couch. Meg brought a bowl of warm water laced with Dettol, and sponged the blood and dirt from the cut and broken face.

Tom Durward turned away. He had no doubt now who Stephen Mallany was. But, as Meg wiped, she seemed to wash years away, and Tom saw revealed the monkey-face of a lively and nervous adolescent. It was like the cleaning of an Old Master, with the grime of years and the varnish once applied to give the paint a glossy surface, now sponged clean to let you see the bright colours or even, sometimes, long-hidden figures emerge.

Tom experienced one of those moments of deceptive déjà-vu. He saw himself wiping that other face, Jamie's, to reveal the colour of death. He hadn't of course done so, except in imagination and bad dreams; someone else had cleaned Jamie up hours before Tom saw his dead body.

"Have you and Stephen fallen out?" he had asked Jamie in that chilly Sunday hotel restaurant the last day they were together.

"Stephen's in trouble," Jamie said, "he's gated."

"What sort of trouble?"

"Just trouble." Tom was sorry to hear that, said so. Stephen had stayed with them in the London flat over Easter, and they had gone to the National. *The Cherry Orchard* or *Uncle Vanya*? Yes, *Uncle Vanya*. But he didn't pursue the matter, which was evidently awkward.

It hadn't been a good day. It rained in the afternoon and they sat in the hotel lounge looking out at dripping azaleas and rhododendrons so wet their leaves seemed to be black. At one point Jamie said, "Do I have to stay on at school?"

Chapter Twenty-Five

He wasn't quite fifteen. "I don't like it," he said.

He drowned himself in the lake ten days later. For the sake of the school, the coroner was persuaded it was an accident.

There was no explanation in the diary Jamie had kept. But then there were no entries for the last fortnight, except a note of that lunch. For years Tom kept that diary with him. He knew it by heart. But it yielded no solution.

He said to Meg, "We ought to get him to hospital."

The funeral was the last time he had seen Stephen.

Meg said, "He's going to sleep now. It's all right, I can look after him. I've done it for Mike often enough."

"It's not your responsibility."

"Oh responsibility ..."

"He might get worse, go into convulsions."

"I'll ring Sol, he's Stephen's sponsor, he'll know what's best, he always does."

Tom lit a *toscano* and stood by the window looking out at the unrevealing block across the street. It was a dull nineteenth century part of the city.

Sometime, in the bad years when he was mostly out of his mind, he'd had a letter from Stephen who was just about to be ordained, a self-indulgent (he thought) confessional letter.

Stephen was writing, he said, because they had both loved Jamie. He himself had been in love with him, still was, but nothing had happened. Jamie wasn't like that. Tom must believe him. But ... but he couldn't forget Jamie and how he had failed him. That was why he was writing now. He wasn't the cause of Jamie's killing himself. But still he had failed him. (He said that three times.) There was another boy in their House, a prefect, who he was sure was responsible. That was all he could say, and maybe he shouldn't be writing at all.

It was a mad confused letter, but Tom was mad and confused himself. He got out the Stowe school list from Jamie's untouched desk in his bedroom in the flat in Cornwall Gardens and pored over it, marking down the names of prefects. He even employed a private investigator to find out what had become of each of them.

But that was all. He should have called on Stephen in the theological college from which the letter had been written, and forced him to give the name. Hadn't that been what Stephen hoped he would do when he wrote the letter? But Tom hadn't dared.

How odd that the sun shone bright, beautifully life-giving on the street below.

For years he had held the thought that you can't ever know other people; not really. If he had known Jamie, the boy would have lived. And if Jamie had known him ...? People, he thought and wrote, can be simple as long as you keep them at a distance. You can have a very clear and certain idea of those for whom you don't give a damn.

Stephen opened his eyes. Tom knew he knew him. He was sure now that Stephen had recognised him at that first AA meeting. Was that why he had gone on this bender? Was he running away from Tom, memories, everything? Well maybe; and maybe he just wanted a drink.

Meg came back from the telephone.

"Sol's coming round."

"Oh good."

He gave Meg a kiss. They talked a little. Sol would be there almost at once. Tom couldn't stay.

XXVI

The sun was hot as Tom descended Via Nazionale towards Piazza Venezia, full of tourists. He went into a bar and telephoned Belinda; he could remember when you had to search several bars to find a telephone that wasn't *guasto,* out of order. She said, "Come round and tell us properly. Sounds grim. It's only ten minutes walk."

Turning into the ghetto he relaxed. He stayed there, almost forty years ago, in this same Via Portico d'Ottavia which for centuries had been at once prison and sanctuary for Rome's Jews, with its gates locked at night to prevent them from roving. He had come for a night and stayed months with two English friends, the girl a Cambridge contemporary. He hadn't seen either for decades. Their marriage, which had danced beautifully then, was long over.

Belinda greeted him with a light kiss on the cheek. She said she would make tea, suggested he join Erik on the terrace. "Then we can talk."

Erik was stretched out on a canvas chair, he wore T-shirt and shorts. In the sunlight the down on his legs, arms and face was the colour of pale honey. He was reading *The Charterhouse of Parma.* Tom liked him better for that, but he still looked a soft boy. He smiled at Tom and set his book aside.

Belinda came out with the tea. She had made a pot and carried it on a tray with bone-china cups and slices of lemon and a little bowl with sugar lumps. She was wearing a cream-coloured dress that stopped just short of her knees. Her feet were bare.

"We've been so lazy today, the pair of us."

"It's been lovely," Erik said, "so peaceful."

"And you've had this horror," she said. "So how is he? We're really grateful to you."

The tea was good, Lapsang. Tom drank some and told them about finding Stephen, the state he was in, how he refused to go to hospital, how Meg said she would care for him, how she had called Sol.

"He was pathetic, all but done in, and afraid, of course."

"But he must go to hospital," Belinda said. "It's not fair on Meg, and I'm sure she doesn't even like him. We should get him into Salvator Mundi – that's the American hospital on Monteverde – they understand alcoholics there. I'll go and call Meg."

Tom leaned over the terrace wall. It looked away from the street, and the sound of the traffic from the Lungotevere was muffled.

Erik said, "Belinda's so good. I don't know where I'd be without her just now. You know I was Stephen's boyfriend, don't you?"

When Tom didn't reply, Erik said, "Do you think I should blame myself for him going on the booze again?"

"It's no business of mine," Tom said, "but the answer is probably no."

"That's what Belinda says but I don't know if she's just trying to make me feel better, so it's good to hear you say so too. You know I was in Al-Anon for years – junior Al-Anon – before I was in AA myself on account of my mother being alcoholic, so I know all the language, all the arguments one way and the other. I mean I've heard them all my life it seems."

He slid the palms of his hands along his thighs.

"Belinda's wonderful, you know, I really think she's my salvation."

Tom thought: you are a self-centred little prick.

He said, "Did Stephen ever talk about a boy called Jamie?"

Chapter Twenty-Six

The boy who had been as relaxed as a cat in the sunshine hesitated. His tongue flickered across his lower lip.

"Hey," he said, "how d'you know that? It scared me, that he called me Jamie when we were ..." he glanced away ... "having sex. He had this photograph and I asked him about it and he told me it was this Jamie and he was dead. Murdered he said, and then he called me by this murdered boy's name. It was creepy, made me feel like I wasn't there, not me myself."

"Jamie wasn't murdered. Stephen was dramatising that. He killed himself. It was a long time ago, in England, when they were both boys, fourteen, fifteen. You don't look much like him. He was blond too but the colouring's different and the build. He shouldn't have called you Jamie though."

"You knew him then?"

"Oh yes, I knew him."

"He wasn't ... your son?"

"Not quite. My nephew, my ward."

"You don't mind me asking? He must have meant a lot to Stephen."

When Tom didn't answer, Erik said, "You don't like any of this, I guess. He must have meant a lot to you too. I'm sorry. I owe something to Stephen, I'm aware of that. I wouldn't have gone with him if I hadn't been drinking, though it was me picked him up, I have to confess. But he got me back into AA and I do hope" – he flashed the smile that had made him a schoolgirls' pin-up a couple of years past when he was a star in a teen soap – "you don't think I'm too young to be a real alky. Mike does. He says I'm to real alkies like him what alcopops are to Scotch. But I know what it's all about – you should have seen my ma and when I felt myself going that way too, saying the same things even, the same crappy awful things – I just knew where I was heading, and no thank you."

"There's no merit in going the length," Tom said. "It's a long, dark, stupid tunnel and you're wise to call a halt."

"Mike says different, he says my pretty ass hasn't come within sight of the gutter and so I'm a phoney. If I'm talking too much it's because I'm nervous. You see I've been stupid. I didn't connect with who you are, didn't cotton on. It was real stupid not to realise it was you wrote the script for *Gehenna*. I just adored that movie – it really hit me. So you see …"

XXVII

"So she's stripping you down, tearing the skin off."

Reynard Yallett kept his tone light, his mockery as friendly as could be. Not truly friendly of course; there was always that undercurrent.

Gary made no reply. They were sitting outside the café in the piazza at the foot of the tree-lined avenue in which Kate had her apartment. She had retired there, on the plea of a headache. Reynard had said that there were matters he must discuss with the Chicken, now as good a time as any.

He summoned the waiter, ordered a whisky for himself, a Diet Coke for Gary.

"Still not drinking? That's sensible. People like you talk when they drink. You don't want to talk, Gary, not you. You might say things you come to regret. So how far has she got?"

Gary picked at skin, right thumb scraping left. He didn't speak till the waiter brought their drinks, but looked away, his eyes on the leather-suited boys who were revving their bikes on the other side of the street.

"Why the fuck are you here?" he said. "We got nothing to discuss."

"Curiosity, chicken, curiosity. I suffer from insatiable curiosity. And this experiment the good Dr Sturzo is conducting – how could I resist monitoring it?"

"You was my brief," Gary said. "That's all. It's over. I got off, didn't I?"

"Thanks to me," Yallett said.

"That's as may be. I don't know myself. Nobody knows. There wasn't the evidence. Need evidence for a conviction, don't you. You pointed that out. I said thank you. I don't owe you nothing now."

"Calm down, chicken, calm down."

"Don't call me chicken. I don't like it. And I'm calm enough. What do you want here? Why're you getting at me?"

"Getting at you, chicken? Getting at my favourite kid killer? What makes you think that?" Reynard Yallett held up his glass to the light, swirling the ice round, and drank half of the large measure. "Are you fucking the good Dr Sturzo?"

"That's disgusting, she's old enough to be my mum. You think I did it then, knifed that nigger."

"I know you did, darling. So what? I just wouldn't be too forthcoming with the good Dr Sturzo, that's all."

"Don't know what you mean. I got off, didn't I? That means I'm innocent, not guilty. It's finished."

"Don't be too sure," Yallett smiled, revealing his canines. "There's talk of abolishing double jeopardy. You know what that is, don't you? There's a proposal to allow the Crown a re-trial if new evidence appears. How do you like that?"

"There's no fucking evidence old or new."

"Oh good then, so we've nothing to worry about," Yallett said. "That journalist, Trensshe you know, thinks differently. But he's wrong then, is he?"

"You're dead right, he's wrong. Wanker."

Two of the motor cyclists, with a revving of Formula One proportions, roared round the piazza. Gary followed them with hungry eyes as they disappeared up the tree-lined avenue.

"Come off it, me old china." Reynard raised his left eyebrow and curled his upper lip – a mannerism that delighted or infuriated his TV following. "Pull the other one. I know you did for him. Doesn't worry me. One fewer of these buggers isn't going to spoil my day."

Gary pushed his chair back. He stood very stiff in his dark suit and white shirt, and he looked Reynard in the face. A nerve jumped in his right cheek and he lifted his hand and touched the bone to hide it or still it. He looked as if he was about to make a speech, but there was nothing to say. Perhaps that was it. The waiter, leaning against the wall by the open doorway into the bar, drew on his cigarette. The tall Englishman in the suede jacket had just made an indecent suggestion. He watched the boy turn away. He recognised him as the *dottoressa*'s young friend. He admired the *dottoressa* and could have told the Englishman there was nothing doing; and quite right too. He approached the table, collected the glasses.

Another whisky, *dottore*?

XXVIII

Seeing Erik deep again in *The Charterhouse*, Tom once more warmed to him, a bit anyway. A boy who read Stendhal ... that was OK. For years Tom kept *La Vie de Henry Brulard* as a bedside book, and for him *The Charterhouse* was the greatest novel ever written. In his drinking days he used to say, "Beats *War and Peace* the way a dry Martini beats a Daiquiri."

There was a triangle in it, formed of people whose desires could none of them be satisfied. What could be truer than that? There was the powerful Count Mosca, unhappy because he had fixed his adoration on the certainly adorable Gina Sanseverina, who herself had eyes only for her nephew, the beautiful, intemperate and unreliable Fabrizio. As for Fabrizio himself, he indulged an agreeably hopeless passion for an angelic and unobtainable girl, but really, Tom thought, was in love first with himself, which in the Stendhalian world was as much as to say, in love with his own vitality, life indeed.

Erik laid down the book.

Tom said, "All right, isn't it?"

"All right? It's wonderful ... the whole atmosphere, it's like music."

"Well that was what Stendhal loved here in Italy, not only the music itself but that life here aspired to the condition of opera, people killing for love, that sort of thing."

Belinda rejoined them.

"Really," she said, "people are tiresome. It's all this sensitivity. I've been speaking to Meg, and then Sol, and Bridget – or rather I got Tomaso who is tiresome but practical in his way. Anyway he's against hospital and sides with Stephen and Meg on that.

Chapter Twenty-Eight

Sol agrees that hospital is essential, and that annoys Meg because she thinks it's a slight on her. Stephen won't budge and has passed out again, and Meg's in a temper, I think, because she's not trusted. Tomaso called her, you see, and said he would take over because he fancies himself as an amateur doctor, and then Bridget came on the phone and spoke in that soft sibilant way she has when she's angry, because she said Meg has been rude to Tomaso. I bet he put her up to it, told her to phone. And Kate's not answering, though she's the one with more sense than the rest rolled up together except Sol. It really is hopeless, I don't know why one bothers."

She flopped into a deck-chair. Erik came and stood behind her and stroked her hair and then began to massage her neck.

"Relax," he said, "it's not like you, this isn't ..."

Who's to say what's like anyone, Tom thought. We make for ourselves impressions of people and if they act in a way that doesn't fit that impression, we say they are acting out of character, as if they were actors condemned to be typecast,

"You've done all you can," Erik said. "Really."

"I've done nothing," Belinda said, "except yatter on the phone and make a nuisance of myself."

XXIX

They talked of going out to a restaurant. "Later," Belinda said, "Meg may call again and I don't want to speak on the mobile, not in a restaurant, not about this."

It got dark, but was still warm and they didn't move from the terrace. Erik set himself, evidently, to please, amuse and interest Tom. If it lasts, Belinda thought, it will always be like this; only it can't last, won't. She fetched another bottle of mineral water from the fridge and filled their glasses. Erik reached up with his and she ran the back of her index finger along the line of his jaw. He was telling Tom about a star of the early sixties, one of the several billed as the new James Dean, who had been reduced to work on Erik's teen soap.

"He was sad and sour. I guess we were all afraid of him. And then I saw *Barbary Shore*, the movie he made from that Mailer novel, and he was electric, just electric. And I thought, he really had it once and then it was for myself I got scared. The way he was all burned up, exhausted, dried out."

Tom took a half-*toscano* from his breast pocket and lit it.

"Talent dies. 'Some seed fell upon stony ground and sprang up quickly and withered because it had no roots.' Maybe he was lucky to be able to work at all."

The telephone rang. Belinda sighed and went to answer.

Erik said, "He didn't for that long. On account of the chick who played my girlfriend. She was just thirteen, but a real little Lolita, I mean, she just set out to ... you know ... she was surely no innocent, but she was great at playing the innocent ... little bitch. There was even talk of prosecution, but her Mom wouldn't have that, thought it would do her little darling –

117

and wage-earner – no good careerwise. Some career; she had talent enough to fry a Big Mac ... maybe. But you know, he just shrugged his shoulders and walked away from it all with a sad sort of hopeless dignity. It could be that was a performance too, but it was a hell of a lot better one than he gave on the set."

Belinda came back on to the terrace.

"That was Kate. We've got to go over there. Or at least I have to. There's trouble. She wouldn't say what, but she was agitated, I've never heard her like that, she's usually so in control." She turned to Tom, "You'll come too, won't you. Please."

"I scarcely know her, but if you think I can be of some help, of course."

"Is it Gary?" Erik said.

"I don't know. I really don't know anything. Just, Kate said come. She sounded desperate."

"Where does she live?"

"Parioli. We'll have to take a taxi. But she said, stop it in the piazza and walk from there. That's odd, isn't it?"

"It's weird," Erik said. "I guess it's to do with Gary."

Belinda spoke into the intercom. "Kate, it's me."

The buzzer sounded. They entered the silent hall and rang the lift. Kate was waiting for them on the landing outside her apartment. She took Belinda in her arms. Belinda hugged her hard.

"You know Tom," she said. "I thought he might be some help."

"I don't know that anyone can. But thank you."

Belinda held her a moment. There was a swelling under her left eye and her upper lip had been cut, was still smeared with dried blood.

"Is it Gary?"

Kate pulled away, led them into the apartment, through the dark entrance hall and into a long-ceilinged drawing-room lit by two standard lamps and an art nouveau electrolier. Immediately under this lay the body of a man. He was face down and wore only a shirt and socks. There was a big red stain on the cream shirt and a small puddle of blood on the parquet floor. It was a moment before Belinda recognised him as Reynard Yallett. She knelt beside him a moment to make sure. Then she got up and looked across the room. Gary was sitting on the window seat. He was in the shadows and there was no expression she could put a name to on his face.

"Tell," she said. "You'd better tell if you're up to it."

"I shouldn't have brought you here," Kate said. "I must be mad. But I couldn't think what else to do."

"He is dead, isn't he," Erik said.

"There's no doubt about that," Tom said. "Do we know who he is? I take it we do."

"Oh yes," Belinda said, "we know. It's Reynard Yallett – the QC. You must have heard of him."

And I came close once to marrying him, she thought. She looked again towards Gary who gave no sign that he had noticed their arrival.

"It's banal," she said, "but I think since we can none of us have brandy we could do with a cup of tea. And then tell. I'll make it."

Erik followed her through to the kitchen.

"You're so cool," he said, "and I'm shaking."

"Getting in a state won't help us."

She plugged the kettle in and turned and kissed him lightly on the lips.

"But I'm glad you're here. Bless you."

Back in the drawing-room Tom Durward said, "I take it you haven't called the police."

119

Kate stayed silent, looked a negative.

"And don't intend to?"

Again she made no reply, sat down in a wickerwork chair, keeping her eyes fixed on the body as if praying for it to move.

"Reynard Yallett," Tom said. "The mills of God ... do you mind if I smoke?"

Belinda, returning, poured tea. Erik took a mug over to Gary and set it beside him, getting no acknowledgement.

"Tell then," Belinda said. "I know it's going to be difficult, but tell."

Erik, turning away from Gary, knocked his foot against an object which skittered across the parquet. He bent down, drew back from the knife which now lay in the open. When he sat himself on the arm of Belinda's chair, he couldn't take his eyes off it.

"Reynard came back," Kate said, "came over, I mean, I don't know exactly when. He'd been drinking. He was in a foul mood. Gary had walked out on him when they'd gone to discuss what Reynard said was some business they had to settle. I don't know what it was. It puzzled me, I couldn't see what they might have to discuss. I wasn't expecting him and wasn't pleased to see him. I showed that and he became offensive, aggressive. I won't repeat what he said, but I slapped his face. It was then he hit me, knocked me down. I may have been knocked out, I don't really know. But the next thing I knew he was on top of me, tearing at my clothes, trying to rape me. I may have screamed, must have. Then he went all limp, just a weight on top of me. I struggled out from under, and he was like he is now. He didn't even know Gary was in the apartment, you see."

All the time she was speaking Gary kept his eyes fixed on the floor. His silence filled the gaps in Kate's statement.

Motor bikes, the neo-Fascist youth at play, screamed down the avenue below. "I guess he was asking for it," Erik said, "but Jesus ..."

"And no police?" Tom said again. "I'd have thought in the circumstances you describe ..."

"I know it sounds crazy," Kate said, "and I'm not thinking straight, I admit that, but the circumstances, other circumstances ... Gary's record, and Reynard has – had – a high profile in England. Am I mad or what? I mean, even if in the circumstances the court was lenient – well, this is Italy, it might be, but how long would Gary spend in jail before any trial? And I got him into it."

"Hardly," Belinda said, "you speak as if it's your fault."

He didn't have to use a knife, she thought, he could have grabbed him by the hair and pulled him off. But what was the point – what is ever the point of listing could haves? "He did it for me," Kate said.

"So, no police. We're here to organise a cover-up," Tom said. "That's it, isn't it?"

"I can't ask you to do that," Kate said, "but then I don't know what I can ask. I don't even know what I want, only what I don't want."

"You're shivering, darling," Belinda said, "and no wonder. But Tom's right. If we're not calling the police, and I see why not, then we've got to ... concoct something. Do you know where Reynard was staying and for how long?"

"The Excelsior. Till tomorrow, I think. He was just here for the weekend. But it's crazy. How if I, we, just leave Gary out of it, and I say I did it, protecting my ... you know what?"

"That's crazy, if you like," Belinda said.

"I don't know," Tom said, "how good the Rome police forensic is, but I would guess good as anyone else's. And the wound would be wrong and the distribution of the blood, and anyhow where did you get the knife at that moment? Just had it to hand? And the questioning, the examination ... chances are you and Gary would both find yourselves under arrest, pending ..." He played with the handle of his stick, and traced a circle on the floor. "Seems to me the body must be moved. Without the body here what is there that connects you and Gary with the crime? Would anyone have seen him arrive?"

"I don't know. The porter goes off duty when the outside double door is locked. At seven. But the other apartments? I don't know. He might have met someone. I just buzzed the door for him."

"There's a fair chance he didn't," Tom said. He put a match to his cigar which had gone out. "Pasolini," he said.

"What do you mean?"

"Pasolini ... you remember, Belinda, the notice on Pasquino. A mysterious death, a crime never solved ... that's what we want."

"I'm lost," Erik said.

"Pier Paolo Pasolini, poet, film director, Marxist, homosexual ... his body was discovered on waste ground on the edge of a housing estate just out of the city. He'd been beaten up, run over by a car, I don't recall exactly. He'd a taste for rough trade and the theory was a pick-up that went wrong. But some – the chap who wrote that *pasquinata* for instance – think it was political with the security services involved, as accessories anyway.

That's irrelevant. But Pasolini presents us with a model, that's what I mean."

Erik said, "Wow, you just thought this up now?"

"You forget, I worked in Hollywood for years. Concocting scenarios is my trade."

"Reynard wasn't queer," Belinda said. "But he was a notorious womaniser, rape not beyond him – sorry, Kate."

"Doesn't matter."

"No," Tom said, "doesn't matter, though I think you'll find he was more versatile."

For a little nobody said anything. Erik, awkward, filled the silence by pouring more tea. Gary hadn't touched his mug.

"You OK, Gary?"

Kate drank tea, lit a cigarette, hands shaking.

"I'm sorry," she said. "I really am crazy, must be. I can't let you all make yourselves accessories. I shouldn't have called you."

Belinda crossed the room to Kate's chair, perched on the arm, stroked her hair.

"It's mad," she said, "but it might work. It could work. And what's the alternative? You owe something to Gary and the only way that debt can be paid is by doing as Tom suggests. If we all get in trouble, well so be it. But I think it may work."

She thought, this isn't me, but what else can we do? How right I was to tell Kate she was mad to have Gary here, because if she hadn't none of this would have happened; Reynard wouldn't have come to Rome. But what does any of that matter – she looked at Erik who was gazing at the body, his lips parted – what does it matter since what has happened has happened? Thank God Tom Durward was with us, but ... he's enjoying this, he is ...

123

"We'll need a car," she said.

"You can't involve yourself in this, Bel," Kate said.

"Oh I think I can, I think I must. Each for each is what we teach, you know."

"I could get Stephen's," Erik said. "I've got the spare set of keys."

"Oh no," Kate said.

"No," Belinda said, "that seems to be taking advantage of him."

"He doesn't have to know. I'm allowed to use it. Least I was."

"But if something went wrong."

"There's no connection between Stephen and ..." Erik pointed to the body.

"No," Tom said. "There is in fact a connection. I won't go into it now, but it's there."

"Steal one," Erik said.

"How?"

"Too risky."

"I could do it. My second stepfather was mad on cars, taught me how to hot-rod most any one."

"No," Tom said. "Belinda's right. Too risky. Hertz is the answer, Hertz and the American Express. I'll see to it. I'll take it for a week, and then when the job's done, drive south and eventually leave it for collection in Naples ..."

"But," Kate said.

"It'll take me a couple of hours maybe. Will you be all right till then? First though I think we should wrap him up. In something you can bear not seeing again, Kate. Sheets? And we'll need polythene – rubbish sacks'll do – to line the boot."

XXX

Silence hung over the apartment like the empty Sundays of Belinda's years as a young woman in London, Sundays when church bells made her feel anxious, afraid of the future, when her life seemed a cheat, drained of pleasure or promise.

It was Kate who roused them from silence now.

"If it's to be done, if this crazy thing is to be done, then let's get it in motion."

She fetched sheets. With help from Erik and Belinda she rolled the body over and wrapped the sheet round it. She got a bucket and swabbed the floor. There was only a little blood, but already a reddish-brown stain appeared through the sheet.

"You'll have to sacrifice another, maybe two," Belinda said. "We don't seem to be much good at this. Needs practice, I suppose."

And all the time they worked to remove evidence of the crime, Gary sat unmoving and – who could tell? – unmoved.

I didn't like Reynard, Belinda thought, in the end I didn't like him at all. I was afraid too. And this is how it ends. She felt Erik slip his hands over her shoulders and rest his face in her hair.

Kate was sitting by Gary speaking to him. Belinda couldn't hear what she was saying. Then he got to his feet and left the room. He passed very close to the body rolled up in the sheets, but he didn't look down at it.

"I've sent him to take a shower," Kate said. "We'll have to dispose of the clothes he was wearing. He knows that of course. He's been here before after all."

"Though you wouldn't think so," Belinda said. "Is he all right?"

"I don't know. I don't know anything."

The doorbell rang.

"It's too soon for Tom to be back. Don't answer it."

"It might be him though."

The ringing was repeated: three short stabbing rings followed by two long ones. "Oh Christ, it's Mike," Kate said. "I know that ring. It's his special ring."

"Then you mustn't answer."

"If I don't, he's capable of ringing every bell in the building. He's done it before. He'll have to come up. It's the least of ..."

"Put him off. Say you're ill. Invent something."

"I'll try. But you know Mike."

In a moment, "He's on his way up, I'm afraid. There was nothing I ... it was that or ... we'd better get Reynard out of sight."

So they hauled the body behind a couch.

There came a banging at the door and Mike's voice howling the presence of the ghost of Roger Casement. Kate hurried to admit him. He stumbled into a heavy embrace.

"A great provoker of lechery," he shouted, and, freeing himself, bouncing off the doorpost, was in the drawing-room where, now, Belinda and Erik sat on the couch. Mike lurched towards them, fell forward trying to kiss Belinda, landed sprawling on the floor, and gripped Erik's leg to help him back to his feet.

"Do sit down, Mike," Kate said, and guided him with difficulty to a chair that gave no view behind the couch.

"It's Belinda," he said, "Belinda and a puffy boy. Got a drink for me, Kate darling? NO? No drink for Mike? But Mike's outwitted you. Prepared." He fished a half-bottle of whisky from his inside breast-pocket, unscrewed it, and swigged. "Be prepared, it's the Boy Scout's solemn creed." He drank again. "And be clean in word and deed."

126

Kate moved to take the bottle from him.

"No point," Belinda said, "you might as well let him have it."

"Wonderful," Mike said. "Belinda has my worst interest at heart. Darling girl."

Kate sighed.

"All right," she said, "I can't stop you. Go ahead and ..." she caught sight of the knife on the floor a few feet away from Mike and, affecting indifference, picked it up. She was standing there with it in her hand when Gary came in, showered, changed into dark-blue shirt and dark suit; he was very pale and clean and looked no more than sixteen.

"It's another puffy boy, a puffy killer if I'm not mistaken. And Mike never is. All human life is here. But where's Reynard, where's the Fox?"

"You've lost me," Kate said.

"Spies everywhere. The Mike Intelligence Service never sleeps. Like the dear old Windmill, we never close."

Kate took the knife through to the kitchen and washed it under the tap. Gary followed her.

"Who is this guy?"

"Mike? Not to worry."

"Oh yeah?"

He made to take the knife from Kate.

"No," she said. "I'll keep charge of this, if you don't mind."

"How come he knows about Mr Yallett?"

"I don't know what he knows."

Mike lay back in his chair, the bottle held in both hands between his legs.

"Hunting the Fox," he said.

"What makes you think Reynard's in Rome?" Belinda said.

Erik squeezed her hand.

Chapter Thirty

Mike shifted his gaze to look at her.

"Like a fuck?"

"I don't think so, Mike."

"Got your puffy boy, Kate's got a puffy boy too, poor Mike."

He raised the bottle.

"Staunch strong defender and my oldest friend, Scotch whisky," he said, and drank. "What's the Pope's telephone number? VAT 69. Joke. Soixante-neuf, how d'you like that, puffy boy?"

Gary said, "Why don't you shut up and fuck off?"

There was a burst of music, the opening bars of Beethoven's Fifth. Mike fished his mobile from his pocket.

"Roger," he said. "No darling it is indeed Mike. Roger's what you say on these instruments. Didn't you see the movie? No, no sign yet, the Fox has gone to earth. What's that? ... Of course I will. Trust Mike ... Why shouldn't you? Why shouldn't you be the last person on earth to do so? ... No, I'm not ... Never fear. The Hunt continues."

He took another drink, put the mobile on the arm of the chair.

"Clarissa," he said.

"Who's Clarissa, Mike?"

"Thin girl. Elastic legs. Works for the paper. Got the hots for the Fox. Asked me to hunt him down. All part of the Mike service. We never close, like the dear old Windmill."

XXXI

Tom Durward reversed to park. Turning his head caused his neck to click and he felt a stab of pain just below the shoulder-blade. Eleven o'clock. They would have to wait a while yet. Traffic was still busy, and there were people on foot coming home from restaurants or the cinema.

Kate met him at the door of the apartment.

"All right so far," he said, a stock phrase recalling that New Yorker cartoon of the man falling from the Empire State building and uttering that sentiment as he passed the fourteenth floor.

She led him into the kitchen.

"We've a complication," she said. "Mike. You know Mike, don't you? I couldn't keep him out. He's drunk which doesn't matter, but he's also looking for Reynard, which does."

"How drunk?"

"Roaring, making no sense. We got Reynard out of sight behind the couch. I don't understand it. Some girl, a journalist in London, has set him to look for Reynard, I've no idea why. She keeps ringing him on his mobile."

"Well," Tom said, "it's too early to move anyway, too many people about still."

"I shouldn't have got you into this."

"Did anyone see him arrive?"

"I don't know. They may have heard him shouting. I should think they did."

"I don't suppose it matters," Tom said.

Mike, focussing on Tom, held the bottle aloft.

"*In nomine patris filii spiritus sancti*, not a drop spilled till it's ten years old."

"How's it going, Mike?" Tom said.

"Like a bomb, never going to be sober again, that's a promise. What have you done with my wife, Durward?"

"She's all right."

"Sure she is. Mike pays the bills and often the poor guy he have no socks."

"Why don't you shut the fuck up?" Gary said.

"Puffy boy. That's what the girls want now, Durward, puffy boys. Find one for Meg, find one for my wife."

"Looking for Reynard, I hear, Mike?"

"We seek him here, we seek him there ... is he in heaven, is he in hell?"

He staggered to his feet, lifted the bottle, drank one, two, three deep swigs, shuddered and collapsed, one hand outstretched still holding the bottle aloft.

Durward took it from his grasp and set it on the coffee table. There were a couple of inches left in it.

"That's that then."

The opening bars of Beethoven's Fifth rang out. Belinda reached over and switched the mobile off.

"With any luck he'll be out for hours," she said.

Erik said, "That bottle makes me nervous. Should I pour it down the sink?"

"Leave it," Tom said. "Poor sod'll need it when he comes to. Kate, are you all right? Is your voice under control?"

"I think so. Doesn't it sound it? Why anyway?"

"Because it might be a good idea if you were to ring Meg, tell her Mike's here. Make it all sound normal. Say Belinda came round and it was lucky she did because Mike got violent. You're going to have a black eye in the morning and this'll account for it."

"Did I call Belinda? Why didn't I call Meg herself?"

"Because Mike threatened to leave if you did and you couldn't risk letting him loose in the state he's in.

If we're lucky he'll have blacked out. Does he have black-outs?"

"He does indeed."

"Fine. Besides Meg's caring for Stephen. You didn't know that of course, but you do now because Belinda called you earlier to discuss his case. All right?"

Kate made the call. Meg was grateful, asked if she should come round, was told there was no point, Mike would sleep till morning, and in any case how was Stephen? Sleeping too but sometimes moaning in his sleep. What a pair. Thanks and thanks and thanks, what we women go through.

They sat, not speaking, listening till there was quiet below, only an occasional car. Erik began to shiver, though the room was warm. Belinda slipped her arm round him.

"What about rigor?" she said. "I wish I'd read more detective stories."

Poor Kate, she thought, but I did warn her. Pointless.

"I think it's time," Tom said.

He gave Erik his stick and sent him to bring up the lift. Then with Gary's help, he got Reynard's body up from behind the couch, and slung it in a fireman's lift over his shoulder. He told Gary to bring Reynard's clothes and the polythene bags, and said, "Gary and Erik'll come with me. We'll drive south afterwards. It's best you stay with Kate, Belinda."

"You'll call?"

"In the morning."

Belinda at the lift door held Erik a moment, feeling his shiver again, and kissed him, firmly, on the mouth. Kate stretched out a hand to Gary but stopped short of touching him.

"It's going to be all right," she said. "Just do as Tom says."

Chapter Thirty-One

They stood watching the lift doors close and then the empty shaft.

"I think we're all mad," Kate said.

In the lift Tom was careful to keep away from the walls in case of bloodstains coming through the sheets. He told Erik to fish the keys out of his pocket, and told him the car's make and registration number.

"Get the boot open and whistle if the street's clear."

"Boot?" Erik said.

"The trunk."

They waited by the big front door, on the latch, till Erik whistled. Gary took the polythene and lined the boot. Then Tom, with a glance up and down the street, stumbling a little on account of the weight, followed them to the car and with Gary's help eased the body into the boot. Rigor was just setting in but they were able to bend the knees and force it into the foetal position. They closed the lid and got into the car. Gary sat in the front beside Tom. Erik sat forward on the back seat. He held Tom's stick upright between his knees and gripped it hard till his knuckles ached. Tom started the engine and headed downhill towards the piazza. A police car roared up the other side of the road.

It was years since Tom had driven in Rome, and once across the river he was unsure of directions. But that didn't matter. He wasn't yet heading anywhere in particular. Everywhere on the outskirts beyond the city there was waste land, stretches of ground which had once been pasture in the *campagna*, but was now full of brambles, pits, abandoned irrigation ditches. Somewhere in that desolate country would do. Meanwhile all that was necessary was to head south and avoid an accident or traffic infringement. At last they got across the *anulare* and beyond the district where the street-lighting was good. There were still blocks of apartment buildings and workshops, but the roads were now pot-holed and dimly lit. Dogs, lean and furtive as if they had seen better days or never a good one, scurried and scavenged.

The road divided. Tom took the left fork where there were no lights, and in a hundred metres or so the road was no more than a farm-track.

"This won't do," Gary said. "Tyre tracks."

You're the expert, Tom thought, though nobody was going to examine every hired car and they would be leaving it in another city. There was no chance this car could be connected with the body whenever it was found, but even if there was no chance, it was wise to take no chance. The words stuck in his head as a refrain.

"I don't want to get too far into the country," he said.

"Why?" Erik asked. "The more remote the better surely."

"I don't think so," Tom said.

"Make it look the wrong sort of killing," Gary said.

They came to a bridge over a little stream. A road ran off to the right following the water. Tom turned into it. A bit along the bank fell away sharply. It was all covered with bushes. You couldn't tell what they were in the darkness. The moon was just rising. Tom stopped the car and they got out. Away in the distance, the sky was yellow and orange with the lights of the city.

"This'll do."

Tom opened the boot and they hauled the body out. It had stiffened some more and for a moment it seemed it was stuck there. They rolled it out of the sheets and it lay at the edge of the road. A shaft of moonlight struck the face, and it looked as if Reynard was working hard to retain the sneer of command he had worn in life.

Gary got his foot under the body and tipped it over. It hung still and he shoved it again. Then it rolled into the bushes. It caught and for a moment stuck still within sight of the road. There was a sound of breaking undergrowth as its weight told, and it went down through the scrub till they couldn't see where it had arrived short of the stream. Gary brought Reynard's clothes from the car, he held up the suede jacket.

"The rest, yes, but kind of what you've planned, they'd never leave this. It's class, expensive."

"All right. We'll dispose of it later."

Gary went through the pockets and handed Tom Reynard's wallet and passport. He took a small tortoiseshell box from the side pocket, opened it, and sniffed.

"Coke."

Tom held out his hand.

"Them that done him wouldn't leave that."

"No they wouldn't," Tom said, and pocketed it.

They stuffed the sheets into the polythene bags, to leave somewhere among rubbish set out for collection.

"Time to go," Tom said, and got into the car.

As he started the engine, a donkey brayed from an invisible yard.

XXXII

Kate said, "I should never have got you into this. I should have called the police, don't you think so?"

She had said it all before, several times, and Belinda thought she might be right. It was collective insanity, what they had done. Nevertheless ...

"There's no turning back," she said.

Neither felt like sleeping. They had removed from the drawing-room which was oppressive, and not only on account of Mike's presence and the foul smell of alcohol he gave off. Kate had thrown the window open before they came through to the kitchen where they were drinking tea.

"Maybe you do owe it to Gary," Belinda said. "I wish you'd never seen him though."

"I don't know what we are going to say."

"That's unlike you," Belinda said, and hoped she didn't sound sharp. She felt sharp but wanted to conceal it. She was sharp because what had happened had changed everything. She and Kate would never again be what they had been. They might be closer but close in a new way. The balance had been disturbed. Kate had incurred an obligation, and Belinda didn't like that.

She was afraid too, not on account of any police questioning. She wasn't ready to be afraid of that, and she might never be when it came about. Her fear was, well, ignoble. What was this night going to do to Erik?

Kate stubbed her cigarette. The ashtray was brimming. She emptied it in a bucket under the sink, poured them more tea and lit another cigarette.

"We should have asked Tom what his plans were for after," she said.

"I don't know. Should we?"

Chapter Thirty-Two

"We don't even know if he was supposed to be here this evening. Or the boys."

"Oh I think they weren't," Belinda said. "But then that may depend on Mike. If he remembers anything."

"It's a bugger," Kate said.

"Yes indeed. We have to play it by ear, I suppose. For now anyway. Tom said he'd telephone."

"So he did."

Silence descended on them, a long trembling silence, forcing them apart, each conscious of the other's otherness. Belinda looked at the clock: 4.20.

"Angels passing," she said; and the silence held again as if each listened for the whirr of wings.

"Damn Reynard," Kate said.

A bit late for that, Belinda thought. But you must stop yourself from beginning to dislike your friend because she found herself in trouble and invited you to share it.

Kate's face was dark and heavy, the swelling under the eye large, purple-black with splashes of yellow. She turned away, looked out of the window, across the courtyard of the apartment block. It was still night, only a couple of windows showed where insomniacs, early risers, were urging on the day. Or perhaps they merely opened on bedrooms whose inhabitants feared the dark.

"It all depends on Mike, doesn't it," she said, echoing Belinda. "I hope to hell he has blacked out. He does black out, you know, goes sometimes all day without memory or consciousness. He's told me as if it was something to be proud of. I never blacked out myself, not even in my worst times. Did you? I can't remember."

"Does it matter?" Belinda said.

"But what if Mike hasn't this time?"

"What indeed."

"Of course he didn't really see anything, that's certain. But ... I wonder where they put it. I wonder when it'll be found."

XXXIII

Tom Durward stepped out of the car and closed the door quietly so as not to disturb the sleeping boys. It was an hour or so after dawn, chill and fresh. Mist was rising from the ground but the hills inland were still shrouded. He would have liked a cup of coffee. He sighed and lit a cigar. Not far off came the sound of a tractor starting up. Someone, he couldn't remember who, a philosopher perhaps, had written that we must judge a man neither by what he says nor by what he writes; and not, Tom thought, by what he does.

Erik joined him.

"I woke up," he said. "I guess I was cold."

"It's colder out here."

Erick stretched, yawning, then smiled.

"This is cool," he said.

"You think so. I've been wondering if we're off our heads."

They hadn't talked as they drove south after dumping the body. Tom had turned the radio on and found some jazz; not good jazz, but jazz. He was aware all the time of Gary staring straight ahead, down the tunnel of the night road, and of Erik shifting in the seat behind as if, by attaining physical comfort, he could still his mind. But there was no physical comfort, and now he had woken up stiff and cold and stretching himself, but smiling.

"When the mist lifts," Tom said, "I think you'll see Vesuvius beyond the city."

"What are we going to do? What's your plan?"

"Very soon to find an open bar where we can get some coffee."

"Are you still writing this like it was a movie script?"

"I don't know what I'm doing," Tom said. "Don't think of me as the auteur. I was just thinking that I haven't thought this out at all, that we've just done what was there to be done, without examining other courses."

"Because there were no other courses?"

"Maybe."

"Cool," Erik said again, and though Tom wasn't sure that the boy had understood him, and couldn't even have said himself what there was to understand, he found himself for the first time really liking him.

"You're enjoying this," he said.

"I don't know. Last night, last night, I was shit-scared, but hey, look at that pink sky ... I've not seen that many dawns, from this angle like. Say, what are we going to do with Gary?"

"Tie a weight round his legs and drop him in the sea."

"Hey, you're joking. You are joking."

"I'm joking. Let's go find that coffee."

They came down through olive groves to a village. Chickens wandered in the street. Grass grew through abandoned tramlines. A sign said, Napoli 35 km, but it was hard to think they were so near the city. The central piazza was not quite deserted. Two old men in dark suits were sitting on the rim of a fountain which no longer functioned. A bell, thin and discordant, was tolling, to summon the faithful to the first Mass of the day. But only three old women, with shawls round their heads, emerged from the houses and shuffled with short steps and downturned eyes to the church behind the buildings on the other side of the piazza. The stone of the houses was pockmarked, and the shutters and window frames had none of them been painted for years.

Chapter Thirty-Three

There was a bar in the square. A woman rolled up the iron shutter. She was barefoot and wore a black dress and dirty apron. Tom parked the car among half a dozen others head-on to the fountain. An old man appeared from a narrow passage leading a donkey with panniers across its back. He was dressed in a black suit and had a black felt hat on his head. His shirt, which was of a faded washed-out blue, had no collar. He didn't look at them but crossed the square with his donkey.

They went into the bar. The woman was swabbing the tiled floor with a mop. She dipped the mop into a bucket of greasy-looking grey water and paid no attention to them. Tom asked her twice if they could get some coffee before she lifted her head, sighed, and nodded.

Gary said he didn't drink coffee, could he have a glass of milk? It was the first thing he had said since they drove away leaving Reynard Yallett's body in the scrub over the stream. When he got the milk he took the glass over to the doorway and stood looking out on the piazza. The old men by the fountain hadn't moved. A yellow dog with its tail curled up over its back sniffed around their feet.

There were some chairs piled up outside the bar. Tom unhooked one and sat himself down. Erik followed suit. Gary continued to stand, now just behind them and to their left, sipping his milk, looking across the piazza and saying nothing. The church bell tolled again. Gary turned into the bar, set the glass on the counter, and, still without a word to the others, crossed the piazza towards a narrow lane beyond which the church tower could be seen, with the bell swinging.

"He's going to church," Erik said.

"Looks like it. Kelly, Belinda said his name is. Irish name. I expect he's a good Catholic boy."

"My first stepfather was a Catholic, at least I think he was. You don't think Gary's going to confess? That's what Catholics do, isn't it?"

"The bell's ringing for Mass, not Confession."

Tom lit a half-cigar, called out to the old woman, asking for more coffee. The bell ceased its ringing. One of the old men by the fountain removed his hat, scratched his head, nodded twice, very slowly, as if acceding to some point his companion had made, then replaced his hat. There was a low hum of traffic from the motorway down below towards the coast. The sun began to shine.

Erik said, "It's crazy but I feel kind of good and happy; that really is crazy now."

Tom said, "Have you got to that point in *The Charterhouse* when Fabrizio is in prison? What is it he says? Something like 'I was always afraid of prison and yet now I'm here I've forgotten I should be sad.'"

"That's cool," Erik said. He smiled. "This is real. I've only ever acted action till now."

Tom drew on his cigar: soft boy, but handling himself well. They were committed to seeing this through, whatever exactly this might be. Meanwhile there was this moment to savour, of morning in a piazza where nothing could conceivably happen, this moment of nothingness in the young morning sun.

XXXIV

Stephen woke to footsteps in the next room. Sunlight slanted through the shutters. He heard the door open and a woman's voice saying she had brought tea and he should try to drink it. Then the telephone rang and he was left alone. He could hear her speaking, but not what she was saying. Then he remembered who she was and where he was, though he didn't know how he had arrived there. In a little he heaved himself round, seized the mug, which he had to hold in both hands, and drank.

Mummy had come to him in his dream and he had been afraid. Fear had brought him to this point. Fear of Mummy with her scarlet mouth and sharp tongue. Mummy whom he adored and disappointed. Mummy who had wanted a son who would be a reproof to Daddy, and got Stephen. Mummy who had adored Jamie when he came to stay and flirted with him. Mummy who had played at Wimbledon and Mummy still snapping the deadheads off the roses in her cottage garden in Wiltshire. Mummy he had run away and away from ...

Fear of school, fear of being found out for what he was, fear of the corridors and changing-rooms and latrines stinking of disinfectant at his prep school where once Tommy Wood and Michael Cream had rolled him in the nettles.

Fear at Stowe, fear of dark horrors in the Palladian beauty, fear most urgently of Reynard Yallett who knew him for what he was.

Brief respite from fear at Oxford and the theological college where what he was was not unusual, and so acceptable. But fear taking over again when he was in Holy Orders, fear of sin, fear of his knowledge that it was in his nature to seek ruin, fear of what he wanted most, these brief and sordid encounters with the flesh, fear of an avenging God, then fear of madness, fear of nothingness, fear of the footsteps in the next room.

"I'm going up on to the terrace. Join me there, Stephen, when you feel well enough."

Meg was writing a letter to her husband. Sometimes she thought this in-house correspondence was the closest they came now to each other. She had a couple of shoe-boxes full of these letters. In the event of Mike ever meriting a biography, that was where the writer should start.

"I've always known you don't like women," she wrote now. "Of course you want us. It's just that you don't like us. You don't like our conversation or what we do and you don't accept that we have a right to live our lives in a certain way. Could be it's only me you don't like. Our values are antipodal. You are all for toughness and death. I am for give-and-take, conversation that isn't just a succession of sour jokes, boasts and sneers. We don't suit. I've known that for a long time. We should split. I've said that before. This time I really mean it. This time I'm going to act on it ..."

She gave the letter to Stephen to read.

"If you can bear to," she said. "I'd like to know what you think. Read it while I make some more tea."

Stephen glanced at the letter. The writing flickered before his eyes. It wasn't his business and he was still shaking and sweating.

When Meg returned with the tea, he said, "I don't really know Mike. We just drink together, but I don't know him. He's always rather despised me, I think."

"Oh, Mike's big on contempt. You're a priest, Stephen, I want your advice."

143

"I'm not a priest of your church; you're a Catholic, aren't you? And I'm a bad priest. I'm not even sure I'm a priest at all now."

"Do you know what Mike'll do with this letter? He'll write me a reply assuring me he loves me, swearing I'm the only woman for him, and if I reject him, he'll kill himself. He'll swear that's what he will do. What do you think of that?"

Stephen got to his feet. He didn't move well. His long legs weren't under control, and he used the parapet to put distance between himself and the woman. He reached the corner of the terrace and leaned against the wall, his back to the city.

"Mike won't kill himself," he said, "whatever you do," and didn't know why he spoke so confidently.

"Thanks," she said. "I guess you're right."

He turned to look away from her.

"Was that Tom Durward brought me here with you?"

"Yes," she said, "you've him to thank."

XXXV

Naples was a city Tom Durward had never known well, but one where he had had fun in his time. Probably few foreigners do know it well, he thought, and even fewer north Italians. But it has points in common with Glasgow, which however I no longer know either now. Thinking of Glasgow, where he had spent a year as a newspaperman on the Express when he was young, even before his first visit to Italy, he thought they should perhaps have brought the body right into Naples and left the car in a place where it would be stolen.

They were sitting now in the Galleria, drinking coffee or, in Gary's case, another glass of milk. It was Sunday and still early, so the Galleria was less busy than it would be on weekdays or at noon. He remembered it as a place where talk soared to the vaulted ceiling like the chatter of jackdaws in a chimney.

"One of the two good American novels of the Second War came out of here," he said to Erik. "Does that interest you?"

"I didn't know that."

"It's called simply *The Gallery* and it's by a sad writer called John Horne Burns. It might be your sort of thing. He was queer and an alcoholic."

"I've never heard of it," Erik said. "Why not if it's that good?"

"He wasn't a stayer," Tom said. "Unless you're very lucky you have to be a stayer to be remembered. And even stayers mostly get run down. Besides he preferred the poor Neapolitans to the American dream. A degenerate, you see."

Erik looked round the Galleria which Tom could have told him Burns had described entering as being like walking into a city within a city, and it seemed to him very splendid.

"It's a great place," he said, "I can see that."

"It's called the Galleria Umberto because it's in its way an expression of confidence in the United Italy, the new kingdom, which actually the Neopolitans detested till they learned to milk it."

They were talking for talking's sake, to make Gary's silence less oppressive. But they were both conscious of it. Erik wondered what Tom planned to do with him. There wasn't much you could do with him, he supposed. Then Tom said he must go telephone Kate as he had promised. Mike might be awake now and it was important to know if he remembered anything.

"Not that it can make much difference. Except that if he knows we were there last night, we must have left Rome later than we would like to say we did. If you see what I mean." Tom was away a long time. The shadows shifted in the Galleria. Two boys passed walking so close together that their hips brushed. The curly-headed one in the pale rippling pink shirt looked long, searchingly, at Erik and Gary, then hooked his arm in his friend's, said something, and both laughed. Erik watched them as they continued their stroll round the galleria and out at its far end. They would walk through the place several times a day. He knew that.

Erik said, "I'm just going to the *tabacchi* over there."

He bought a packet of Marlboro, two postcards, a stamp for the USA and one for the internal post.

When he returned to the table, Gary got up. Without looking at Erik or saying anything – and indeed he had not directed a single remark exclusively to him since they met – he walked away, out of the Galleria and into the sunlight of the city.

146

Erik stuck the stamp for the USA on a postcard of the Bay of Naples and wrote his mother's address in California.

He smoked a cigarette. "Naples is cool," he wrote. "I'm OK, hope you are. Be good. Love E." Then he added below a line of kisses, "Hope you're missing me a lot."

The other postcard was for Belinda, and for a little he didn't know what he could say that he wanted to say. He still hadn't written anything when Tom returned.

XXXVI

Kate moved heavily across the room to answer the telephone. It's just lack of sleep, Belinda thought, I must look a bag myself. But it was more than that, and worse. In the reluctance of the stocky body, she saw something broken in Kate. We've acted as if we were free, and our freedom is a prison. There are moments from which there is no turning back; what's done cannot be undone. I wonder if Erik is thinking of me.

"That was Tom. They've got rid of it, they're in Naples."

"So?"

"They stopped in a village and Gary went to Mass. Do you find that extraordinary?"

"Do you?"

"I can't decide. I wish Mike would wake up. I told Tom there was nothing we could fix till we know if Mike remembers anything. Do you think he will?"

Belinda looked away, across the courtyard, to where a woman was watering the geraniums in a window-box.

"I've no idea. How could I have?"

"Of course I'm worried about Gary, I feel responsible. He has a grudge against the world. Why shouldn't he have? But I thought I could lift it."

"Did you really think that?"

"Did I? I don't know. That was my intention anyway. I'm sorry for him now we've made it worse. I began in a spirit of scientific detachment, or so I thought. It makes me ashamed."

Belinda found nothing to say to that.

"How did Tom seem?"

"Cheerful. At ease. As if action was its own reward. Perhaps it is."

"I wouldn't know."

148

"No, we wouldn't know."

"And Erik? Did he say anything about Erik, how he's handling it?"

"He said, soft boy but behaving well."

"That's patronising."

"Yes, it's patronising. I don't know that I really like your Mr Durward."

"He's not my Mr Durward. But where would we be now without him? You've got to admit that."

Sounds of movement came from the next room. The door opened. Mike stood there, smiling.

"Ah," he said, "so this is where I am. Mike, I said to myself, where have you landed this time? On my feet I see. With my two favourite women, who can understand the importance of a drunkard's life."

He sat at the table, raised the half-bottle which he had found by his head when he woke, and drained it, shuddered and said,

"*In nomine patris, filii, spiritus sancti.* So what is the entertainment for the day?"

Belinda sighed. She experienced boredom, irritation. It was wrong of course, or, if it wasn't, she should give the irritation words, for Mike's good and hers. Don't bottle things up: admirable, futile advice. Bottling things up was her nature, and also what she'd been reared to do. A question of manners. Giving vent to your feelings was common. But now, one alky to another, she should do what was necessary for Mike. That would benefit her too: reinforcement. But she was short of sleep and the look of self-satisfaction which drunks wear even in moments of inner misery, provoked by their certainty that their feelings are all that matter ... no, she had had enough of it.

Kate said, "You should call Meg."

Chapter Thirty-Six

"Call Meg? I think not. Meg's the last person I want to speak to. You should know that. She always is. You wouldn't have a beer handy?"

"No, I wouldn't."

"Sad," Mike said, "sad, very. Means I must leave you, sally forth. The human frame cries out for beer."

"Call Meg first."

"Call Meg never."

He rose, paused, looked round the kitchen, then stared at Kate, his expression that of a puzzled child.

"Aren't you going to try to talk me out of it?"

"What's the use?"

"Then I'm lost, really and truly lost."

"Oh bugger off, Mike. Stop your play-acting. Bugger off and drown yourself in beer." Kate followed him out of the apartment, watched the lift descend.

"I played that wrong, didn't I," she said to Belinda.

"Oh, I don't know."

"He's going to wonder why I didn't try to stop him. I am his bloody sponsor after all."

"We're not saints. He'll just think you're fed up with him. He must be used to that by now. What matters is that he clearly doesn't remember anything about last night, not even that he came hunting for Reynard. It couldn't be better, given how bad it might have been."

"Damn Reynard," Kate said. "He really was asking for it, you know."

"Oh quite. I'm sure he was. Rather a pity Gary was here to answer his call, that's all."

"Would you rather he had succeeded in raping me?" Kate said.

"No of course I wouldn't have wanted that."

"Well, then ... I owe Gary something now."

"Yes, I suppose you do."

XXXVII

"So we go south," Tom said.

It was late afternoon. Tom had spoken twice to Kate. Nothing was happening in Rome. Mike remembered nothing. There was no report of the body being found.

"Bit early for that, even if it has been," Tom said.

They were back in the Galleria. It was cool there and at this hour noisy as a flock of starlings.

"So we go south," Tom repeated.

Erik watched the boys he had remarked earlier as, again, they circled – cruised? yes, certainly – the Galleria. The one in the pink shirt caught his eye and smiled. Erik looked away.

"But you ought to call Belinda," Tom said.

"I suppose I should."

"You know you should."

Tom reached for his stick and limped off in the direction of the newspaper kiosk. Erik lit a cigarette. His hand was shaking.

"You OK," he said to Gary, not looking at him.

"Why wouldn't I be?"

The boy in the pink shirt was now leaning against the marble wall across the Galleria. His right leg was drawn up behind him, the foot resting on the wall. He kept his eyes on Erik. "Yes, I really should call Belinda."

"You and her," Gary said. His tone was colourless but Erik read disgust in it.

"Don't see why you're here," Gary said. Then, "He was asking for it, you know that, he was asking for it, the stupid fucker."

"Sure," Erik said, looking at the boy in the pink shirt smiling at him.

"Sure," he said, "he was asking for it, that's why we're here."

They left Naples before dark, drove for three hours on the *autostrada*, then turned off into the hills and came to a small town. Erik didn't catch its name on the signpost. They found a hotel. There were two rooms available.

"Spin a coin to see who shares, if you like," Tom said.

"No need," Erik said, "Gary and me'll share, it looks more natural. OK, Gary?"

Over the spaghetti, Tom said, "I first came south almost forty years ago, my first time in Italy. It was on account of a book about Calabria. You won't have heard of the author but he still had a reputation then, in some circles. Can't read him now, but then I thought it was wonderful. Calabria was very poor then, very beautiful but very poor and very hard. I spent two months down here, walking mostly. Maybe it's a mistake to return. But maybe not. At my age revisiting places you were happy in is one of the remaining pleasures, even if it turns out to be a mistake. Better to make mistakes than to sit doing nothing, feeling sorry for yourself. What do you think? Where've you been happiest? Erik? Gary?"

To Erik's surprise Gary answered. "My mum used to take me to Brighton. For the day like. That was all right. You weren't bothered by nobody at Brighton. We used to go to the races or the beach and then on to the pier. For ice cream. I was just a kid then."

"Used to like Brighton myself," Tom said, "one of the better places in the sad islands". He pushed his plate aside, fetched a half-*toscano* from his breast-pocket.

"Norman Douglas, who wrote that book about Calabria, used to say, his philosophy of life, 'Do what you like and take the consequences.' What do you think of that, Gary?" Gary touched his cheek with long fingers; to stop a nerve twitching?

"You're not getting at me," he said. "We wouldn't be here if you were getting at me. Yeah, you take the consequences, but if you're smart, you dodge 'em. That's what we're doing now, intit?"

"I guess it is," Tom said, and pulled hard on his cigar. "But then the consequences can't always be identified. There's more than one sort of consequence. What you do may change you. That's a consequence which isn't always immediately recognised."

"Don't know about that," Gary said.

Erik said, "I never called Belinda. I'll do it now."

Outside in the little piazza, deserted in the darkness that was broken only by two dull yellow street-lights, he dialled her number on his mobile.

"Are you all right?" she said. "I've been worried. I shouldn't have let you go with them. I don't know why I did. I can't see that it was necessary. But at the time …"

"It's OK," he said, "it's really OK, it's even cool."

"I don't know about that. Still … be careful. Come back soon."

"How about you?"

"Oh me …"

"And nothing's happening, that's what Tom says Kate says."

"Not yet, but it can't go on, nothing happening I mean."

"It's just that it feels distant, like it never happened. That's crazy sure, but it's how I feel. We're in this cool little town where it seems like there's nothing."

"Be careful," she said again. "Miss you."

Did he hesitate?

Chapter Thirty-Seven

"Miss you too," he said.

In their room which was dimly-lit by a low-wattage bulb hanging without a shade from the centre of the ceiling, a room with awkward pieces of heavy dark-stained furniture, a basin but no shower, Gary leaned with his elbows on the windowsill, looking out, in a silence broken only by the barking of distant dogs, while Erik stripped to his Calvin Klein briefs, brushed his teeth, flapped cold water on his face and neck, and got into the big bed and over to the wall side. When there had been talk of sharing, nobody had said there was only one bed in the room.

For a long time Gary did not move, and Erik lay very still wishing he had a book. But even if he had one he knew he wouldn't be reading but only pretending to. Then he closed his eyes as if by doing so he could persuade Gary to forget he was there. It was cool, this, as he'd said to Belinda, like being in a movie, and he'd make use of it when he resumed his acting career whenever that was, soon maybe.

Gary turned from the window and took off his jacket and hung it on a hook on the back of the door. He switched off the light, sat on the only chair in the room and kicked off his shoes and leaned forward to remove his socks. He positioned himself so that his back was to Erik and took off his trousers, and as he hung them over his jacket on the hook, the moonlight played on his pale legs. Then he crawled into bed. He lay well apart from Erik, on his back.

"I know you're not asleep," he said. "Don't touch me, just don't fucking touch me."

He turned over so that his face was pressed into the pillow, which they had to share, it being a bolster.

XXXVIII

Belinda had woken tired. She took her tea on to the terrace and watched the swifts hurling themselves across the sky. The telephone rang. Meg.

"Stephen's intending to go home. Do you think that's all right? So soon? Should I let him?"

"He's a grown man."

"Is he? Are they, any of them? Grown-up, men I mean."

"Perhaps not. Tell him to call me. Say I'll go round this afternoon. All right?"

"All right. Thanks."

"Any word of Mike?"

"No. And that suits me fine."

Stephen, Belinda thought, take him to the meeting tonight, good for both of them. Telephone still in hand, she dialled Bridget's number, then Sol's, spoke to both briefly, reassurances exchanged. Neither had heard from Mike. Ought to call Kate next, didn't. Ashamed of that, nevertheless it was Erik's mobile she dialled, and held her breath till he answered, then found her voice strained. They said nothing that mattered, but speaking was good. When would he be back? She couldn't bring herself to ask that.

She showered, spent time on her face, dressed, and left the apartment to walk, slowly, to Campo de' Fiori, to the bar where the young girl who knew her and admired her served tables in the morning. They exchanged the small coin of the day. She drank her espresso and mineral water. It was still morning-cool. The smell of cut melons came to her from the stall across the way. Two Germans consulted a map and their guide-book at the next table. An old man shuffled past with a Siamese cat on a lead. The buzz and clamour of the market were restful. She lit a cigarette. The Germans argued about whether one day would suffice for the Vatican.

Sol came by, carrying a string-bag with fruit and vegetables in it. He took the other chair and ordered a *caffè doppio con acqua calda*. He had lived in Rome ten or twelve years, but didn't have more Italian than he needed for cafés, restaurants and the market.

"Amelia's working this morning," he said. "So I'm on the shopping rota. You are coming to the meeting tonight?"

"I think so."

"Only think?"

"No, I'm sure."

"We need them, you know. No matter how secure, how well things are going."

He began stuffing his pipe. When he had got it lit, he said, "Just think, we might not be sitting here at our ease. We might be planning the next drink. We're fortunate not to be."

Belinda knew that when Sol spoke like this he was worried about something. She waited. The sun was climbing. She took a floppy cotton hat from her basket.

"I called Kate," he said. "Have you spoken to her today? She sounded a tad agitated."

"No. I tried to call her," she lied, behind her dark glasses, "but it was engaged."

"She takes too much on herself," Sol said. "Bridget was telling me about this young man, her latest project. It had me worried, Bridget too, which was why she spoke of it. We're damaged, vulnerable people. Kate sometimes forgets that. I hope she hasn't overestimated her strength. It's easy to do that. I've got a lot of time for Kate. So has Bridget. Well, you know that."

He drank his coffee, message delivered.

"Is Tom Durward still in town? I was interested to meet him. Time was I used to hear a lot about him. That was when I was on the *New Yorker*."

He smiled. He was a long way down from the *New Yorker* now, made his living or part of it by novelising movies or ghosting the autobiographies of second-grade stars. He wasn't ashamed of this. High literary aspirations, he'd been known to say, had come close to killing him. One reason we drink is our inability to accept ourselves as we are, at our true worth.

"How's Erik?" he said.

Sol, she thought, knew everything. Maybe it was the Talk of the Town pages he worked on at the *New Yorker*.

"He's out of town for a few days."

"Nice kid. He's learning there are other people in the world."

"Oh, I think he knows that."

"You do? Good."

He puffed on his pipe, screwed up his face against the smoke, smiled as if willing Belinda to say more.

"Meg says Stephen's going home. I'm not sure that's wise."

"Yes," she said.

"I called round yesterday. He's still confused, thinks if he could sort his mind out he wouldn't be impelled to drink. We both know that's no good. Try to get him to see that. Bring him to the meeting tonight. He listens to you."

"I'll try," she said, meaning it.

"Must go. I'm on cook rota too. Come to lunch. The girls were saying the other day it's a long time since they've seen you. They're great admirers of yours, but I guess you know that."

"Sweet of them, but not today, Sol, thanks."

It was perhaps what she needed, a friendly domestic lunch with Sol's family, the three beautiful daughters. But it was also, at this moment, precisely the last thing she wanted. So instead when Sol left her she walked, through Piazza Farnese and then along the Via Giulia, keeping in the shade of the high walls, then turned to the right, through narrow streets, walking at random, even now after years not always certain exactly where she was until without ever having formulated the intention she found herself in Piazza del Popolo where she bought a Daily Telegraph, settled herself at a table outside Rosati's and ordered a chicken sandwich and mineral water. There was an article by Kenneth on the op-ed page, subject Britain – American or European? Remembering Kenneth and how he was when they had that one time gone to bed in the afternoon in the old North British Hotel in Edinburgh, so long ago now, Kenneth being then Erik's present age or even less, she was impressed to find him where he was, writing, she supposed, with assured authority. Supposed, because she merely remarked his name, didn't trouble herself to read what he had written. It had been a mistake that afternoon.

It was past two o'clock, the piazza as quiet as it would be at any daylight hour.

"Hi there!"

It was Mike. He had got himself shaved and was near sober. He sat down, snapped his fingers at the waiter and called for a beer.

"Just the one," he said, "the necessary therapeutic one. I've had a morning. On the telephone. Work, the drunkard's last friend. Oscar was wrong, you know. Work's the salvation of the drinking classes."

"Have you seen Meg? Spoken to her?"

He shook his head, gave her his knowing naughty boy's smile.

"Meg doesn't want to see me. She's had enough. Who can blame her? Kate too. Same goes for her. I'm on my own, my ownio, best that way I think."

"Up to you, Mike, but I think you're wrong."

"Not wrong. Been out of it, but Mike's himself again. I'm on Foxy's trail. Old Reynard. Have you seen him, Bel?"

She picked up her pack of Gitanes and lit one. She blew out smoke.

"Reynard?" she said. "I haven't spoken to Reynard for more years than I care to think."

"He's gone missing. AWOL."

"So?"

"London's worried. Paper I write for. Girl on the paper really."

"Run out on her, has he? That was always his style. He's probably holed up with another one."

"Maybe, maybe not. He came to Rome Saturday, didn't return. Had a date with this girl, finish an interview, she says. She's been ringing him about it, can't get hold of him."

"Doesn't sound very unusual."

"But it's a mystery. He had lunch with Kate on Saturday, doesn't seem to have been seen since. You know he defended her puffy boy murderer, don't you?

"As I understand it, Reynard got him off. Innocent. At least not guilty."

"I've been to his hotel. The Excelsior. He hasn't checked out, they told me that, but nobody's seen him since Saturday. Odd, isn't it?"

"Oh," she said, "I expect there's a perfectly simple explanation. There usually is."

XXXIX

I ought to call Kate, but ... I want to call Erik, again. It's ridiculous, I've never known him to say anything interesting. He might say the same of me. It's his skin and his smile and ... and there's thirty years between us. Wherever I look I see him.

Her mobile rang.

"Kate? I was just going to call you."

"We've got to talk."

"Has something happened?"

"Not on the phone. Are you at home? I'll come over."

"Do. I promised Sol I would collect Stephen and take him to the meeting. But there's plenty of time. See you."

She fed the cats, put away the faxes Kenneth had sent which were still lying where Erik had dropped them. She didn't want Kate to know how curious she had been. There was a T-shirt of Erik's on the terrace. She pressed it to her face. It still smelled of the boy. She took it through to her bedroom and laid it on the pillow where his head had rested.

"I'm mad," she said, aloud. "Every bit as mad as Kate."

She sat on the terrace and read in his copy of *The Charterhouse*:

> Shortly after Fabrizio's departure for France, the Countess, who without admitting it to herself, was already beginning to let her thoughts dwell on him a great deal, had fallen into a profound state of melancholy. All her occupations seemed to her to lack pleasure, and, if one may venture to say so, savour. She told herself that Napoleon, wishing to attach the Italian people to himself, would make Fabrizio his aide-de-camp. 'He's lost to me,' she exclaimed, weeping. 'I shall never see him again! He will write to me, but what shall I seem to him in ten years time?'

160

Nevertheless she couldn't wait for the boy to return.

Kate's appearance alarmed her. She had lost the air of competence which Belinda had always found so agreeable. She looked like a widow who didn't know what to say to her husband's friends at his funeral. Belinda even wondered if she had been drinking.

"What is it? Have they found it?"

"No, there's no word of that. I almost wish there was. I woke this morning from a dream in which they had kept it in the boot of the car and were driving it around the Mezzogiorno. Have you got a cigarette? Thanks."

"So what is it?"

"Does the name Philip Trensshe mean anything to you?"

"Should it?"

"He's a journalist. He wrote about Gary's case. What he wrote was instrumental in getting the police and the Crown Prosecution Service to pull the stops out. Don't ask me how that was. It doesn't matter. His father's an MP by the way, but only a Lib Dem. It's the son we've to worry about."

"How come?"

"He called me this morning, full of questions about Gary. I wanted to put the phone down on him but I didn't dare. Do you think he'll have thought that strange?"

"Will he? Why should he?"

"Well, I would in his place. Why should I submit to his questioning?"

"But you didn't say anything?"

"I said a lot. Of course I did. I had to. But that's not all, not even the worst. This Philip Trensshe has a partner, a girl on one of the Sundays. Seems she's in the middle of a piece about Reynard and has been trying to make contact with him."

"I know about her. She's the girl Mike's been speaking to. Here, let's have some tea. It'll do you, do us both, good."

It wasn't like Kate, she thought. Perhaps this is what happened when you made control so important, and then found it slipping away.

"You've seen Mike, then?" Kate said when Belinda brought out the tea. "How is he? He doesn't remember anything, does he?"

"We don't need to worry about Mike, he's buoyant, almost sober. He's working, or thinks he's working, chasing up Reynard for this girl. And he feels good about it, but he doesn't know anything."

"Trensshe and the girl are flying here tomorrow, or the next day, I'm not sure which, if Reynard hasn't surfaced, as he put it. I think they suspect something's up. And when they have asked around and discovered Reynard hasn't been seen since Saturday they'll go to the police. I'm sure they will."

"Did he say so?"

"Not in so many words, but ..."

"But there's no body. Till they find the body, the police aren't going to be interested. Why should they be?"

"Well ... I suppose it's because I feel guilty that ... I don't know."

"For heaven's sake," Belinda said. "'Is no business of ours, *signore*.' That's what they'll say. If a middle-aged English barrister chooses to go off somewhere without a word, well then ... they'll just shrug their shoulders. As for young Mr Trensshe, all you need tell him is what I suppose you may have told him already: that you didn't see Reynard after your lunch with him."

"Yes, but Gary and he went to a bar then. He said he had legal business to discuss with him. And Gary was away for hours ..."

"So?" Belinda said, "so what? What does that matter? We know he didn't kill Reynard then ..."

"We know. But will anyone else believe it when the body is found? Of course Gary had no motive, until ... I mean, Reynard defended him. But ... we don't know anything about Reynard's movements between the time Gary left him and he came drunk to my apartment. What a mess it is."

"If Gary left him at the bar ..." Belinda said, "that would let him out, wouldn't it? Do you know which bar they went to?"

"No, but in Parioli, I'm sure of that. Probably the one I usually go to, I mean, Gary's been there with me."

"Well, next time you speak to Tom, get him to ask Gary. Then, if the answer's right, you can put Trensshe on that scent. The waiter might remember."

"I'll think about it," Kate said.

She crossed the terrace and leaned over the wall, looking away.

"There's another thing."

"Yes?" Belinda said.

"Yes?" she said again.

Still with her back turned Kate said, "Gary needs an alibi. He wasn't at my apartment that evening."

"I thought the whole point was that Reynard wasn't there either."

"Yes, but ..." Kate said, "can we have been here, Gary and me, having supper with you and Erik and Tom Durward before they set off? I've been thinking, you see, it would be good if we could say they had left in the afternoon, but that's not possible because Hertz will have recorded the time Tom hired the car. But if we were all here, and they left for the trip on a sudden whim, well, do you see?"

"Oh yes," Belinda said, "I see. All right, only the more lies we tell, the more likely it is ... never mind."

Pull one card away from a house of cards and the whole thing collapses. That's what she thought.

XL

They drove for two days, without destination in mind, stopping to stroll in small towns and villages, some of which Tom Durward recalled from his journey forty years ago, though more often his memory was obscure. They spoke little. Gary's silence inhibited Erik; there was much he would have liked to ask Durward, felt himself restrained. Yet there was something peculiarly satisfying in this excursion into limbo. Reality was set at a distance. When Tom called Kate and learned that there was no news of the body being discovered, or at least of any discovery having been reported, Erik's sense that this was time out sharpened. The battery of his mobile was exhausted; he welcomed the excuse not to call Belinda, whom, nevertheless, he thought of often with tenderness and embarrassment. He watched Gary intently whenever he thought he wasn't observed.

On the second evening they drove down into Cotrone and found rooms at the Hotel Pythagoras.

"A local worthy," Tom said. "Not the mathematician, the philosopher who taught the transmigration of souls."

It was sunset. In the distance they could see clouds piled above the mountains of the Sila, and heard the rumble of far-off thunder. Rain darkened the hills but the town itself was dry, only a wind blowing up eddies of dust. It was the hour of the *passeggiata*. Girls walked arm in arm on one side of the square, eyed by the boys and young men who congregated round the fountain.

There was nothing to do but watch. Tom bought a local paper; English-language ones were not available.

When they had eaten and Tom and Erik had ordered coffee, Gary wiped his lips with his napkin and crossed the square towards the sea. So soon, this now seemed like a habit, a necessary part of the routine of their days.

Erik said again: "I'd like him you know, if he'd let me. It's hard to think of him ..." he lowered his voice ... "as what he is."

"No mark of Cain? Did you expect to see one?"

"Not exactly like, but ..."

"'There's no art / to find the mind's construction in the face ...'"

"You're laughing at me."

"Not at all."

"Well, then ..."

"People aren't all of a piece. You're an actor, you should know that. And whether they should be judged by what they do is an open question."

"Have you ever known a murderer," Erik said, "before now?"

"Yes," Tom said. He put a match to his cigar before continuing. "Two certainly, and perhaps three. The third was to my mind the worst. The first, he was a poor thing in the village in Scotland where I grew up. I knew him because he had become a sort of dependent of my mother's. He lived in a caravan in the lane behind our house, and he did some garden work for my mother. He'd killed his father, a long time before, when he was little more than a boy, and had been adjudged insane and imprisoned in the lunatic asylum twenty miles away. Eventually he'd been released and my mother, who had known his mother, when they were young, took pity on him and indeed provided him with the caravan. I doubt if he would have survived otherwise. He was a poor thing who never spoke above a whisper. Institutionalised, I suppose they would say now. But the gentlest being you could imagine. I never knew why he killed his father, it was a long time ago."

"And the second?"

"Oh the second was more dramatic. He was an actor in a play of mine and he stabbed his wife, right there on the stage. Actually he was supposed to do that, it was in his part I mean, that he stabbed the actress who was playing his wife, and was indeed his wife, but nobody expected him to use a real dagger. That wasn't how I wrote it."

"What happened to him?"

"Oh he's in prison somewhere, I think he is anyway, a French prison – it was in a performance in Bordeaux."

"Were you in the theatre yourself," Erik said.

"No," Tom said, "I don't follow my plays around, not that closely. But I had known him and liked him. The wife was a sweet girl, but, they said, congenitally unfaithful. He certainly thought so. Rather a mess."

"And the third? You said there was a third."

Durward called the waiter, instead of answering, paid their bill, picked up his stick and said, "Let's walk a little before bed."

The streets were emptying. They could hear their own footsteps. They walked, like Gary, in the direction of the sea, and came down to the beach, deserted, not even a dog. There was a night chill in the air, and in the distance they could see the light shine from the lighthouse on Capo Colonna.

Tom said, "The third? Yes, your friend Stephen knows as much as I do about him. More perhaps. He called you by my nephew's name, Jamie, you said. A dead boy, a boy who killed himself. There's no doubt that he did. But he was driven to it by an older boy, which is why this third murderer, second in time, was the worst of the three. And now he's dead in his turn. The mills of God grind slowly but they grind exceedingly small."

"The mills of God?" Erik said. "I heard you say that before, at Kate's ... You mean?"

"Yes," Tom said. "It would be slander if he was still alive, but you can't slander the dead. I don't know exactly how – I intend to ask Stephen when we're back in Rome, but I know as certainly as I know anything, that it was Reynard Yallett drove Jamie to kill himself. It's not only Kate who owes Gary a debt."

XLI

Kate found herself unable to work. She listened to the tapes she'd made of her conversations with Gary, doing so in case there was anything which it would be prudent to destroy. But there wasn't. There wasn't indeed much of interest. She had failed. Evidently she couldn't continue with him, no matter what happened. It was impossible their relationship should be professional. Indeed it was impossible that there should be any sort of one at all. That was clear. But what was to be done with him, or for him? Perhaps Tom Durward would have a suggestion.

Last night at the meeting Belinda had occupied herself entirely with Stephen, who sat hunched, silent, trembling. Had she lost Belinda too? That was possible. Damn Reynard. And now these journalists ...

She had hesitated when they suggested coming to her apartment. Why should she let them impose on her? But mightn't that seem more natural than suggesting a neutral meeting place? On the other hand if she fixed to meet them in a café, she would be able to get up and walk away. But would that make them suspicious? In the end she agreed that they should come to her. Trensshe probably hoped to find Gary there.

They arrived with Mike in tow. She hadn't expected that.

"Mike's one of our stars," the girl Clarissa said, "we're always hoping he'll write more for us. The piece he did last year about that English bullfighter was the best thing we published in the last twelve months."

She had one of these little girl baby voices Kate had always despised: a Jackie Kennedy of the English suburbs, and the huge dark glasses she affected were simply absurd.

Chapter Forty-One

She said, "I loved your book about that Dutch Nazi, it was really ironical."

"Oh, did you think so? Belgian actually. Kind of you anyway."

Trensshe wasn't what she'd imagined, being fat and balding rather than lean and hirsute. He stuck his index finger in his handkerchief and ran it round his neck, inside his open collar.

"I have to say," Kate said, "I still don't understand how you think I can help you."

"You're the only lead we have," Trensshe said. "We know Reynard Yallett flew out to see you and Kelly. I have to say – I believe in being frank – that I utterly disapprove of the idea of you writing a sympathetic book about Kelly. I think that's what you are planning. In my view he's nothing but a murdering toerag."

"So I'm glad you're not my agent," Kate said.

"Don't let's get sidetracked," Clarissa said. "I mean, that's all so irrelevant, Phil, I've told you that. The question is what's become of Reynard?"

"Why're you so interested?" Kate said, and hoped it came across as offensive. "I don't understand your connection with him."

"Steady on," Mike said. "We're worried, that's all, it's natural. He seems to have vanished off the face of the earth."

"Well, as I said on the telephone, I don't see that I can help you."

"But you had lunch with him, you and," Trensshe paused, "Kelly."

"Certainly we did. Why not? I've known Reynard for years. I was a barrister before I became an academic, we were in Chambers together, it seems a life ago. And as you know, he defended Gary."

"What then?" Clarissa said. "It really is important, you know."

Tell as much of the truth as you can, Belinda had said; the more lies we tell the more complicated it all gets. But don't we want to complicate everything, she had said, to be awkward? No more than is necessary, Belinda said.

She sighed.

"I've told Mr Trensshe all this."

He was standing where Reynard had lain. He would have been astride the body if the body had still been there.

"But I don't mind repeating. We took a taxi back to Parioli. Reynard said he had something he wanted to discuss with Gary. Don't ask me what, because I don't know. He wanted to go to a bar – I don't keep drink in the apartment. So I dropped them in the piazza at the bottom of the road. I suppose they went into one of the bars there. There are three. You could ask. In a little Gary came back here. He went to his room and lay down, if you want to know."

"Why do you keep calling the little toerag Gary?"

"It's his name, isn't it?"

"You speak as if you like him."

"I do rather, actually. He has good manners." Better than yours, Mr Trensshe, she almost added. "Better than Reynard's I might say," she said. "Not that that's difficult."

"Aren't you worried about Reynard?" Clarissa said.

"No, why should I be? I repeat, I don't understand your concern. He probably picked up a woman and is holed up with her somewhere. That used to be his style, I can't imagine he's changed."

Did the girl flush? Was her interest personal, not professional? And did Trensshe who had called himself her partner know that? These were questions Kate would have liked answered.

"Look," she said, "look, Clarissa, isn't it, maybe you're fond of Reynard. I'm not, I never was. He's amusing and good company, but also a shit, always has been. But if you're worried – then, though I can't share your anxiety, my advice is to go to the police."

"We've done that, this morning," she said.

"And?"

"They were useless, simply not interested."

"Well, there you are," Kate said.

"I want to speak to Kelly."

"I'm afraid you can't"

"Oh and why not?"

"Two reasons," Kate said. She was beginning to enjoy herself, which was easier, since Trensshe was every bit as easy to dislike as she had thought he might be ... "First, after the things you've written and the part you played in getting him put on trial, it's unlikely he wants to speak to you; and of course there's no reason why he should do so. It's not yet compulsory to speak to the Press – or have I missed something? And, second, he's not here, he's out of town."

"Why?"

"I'm afraid I don't see that that's any of your business."

"Now, now," Mike said. "Birds in their little nests agree."

"I'm sorry, Mike, I don't like your friend's manner. Mr Trensshe, I think it's time you left. I repeat, Clarissa, I'm sorry if you are worried about Reynard, but there's nothing I can do to help."

"I know something's happened to him, I just know, something awful."

"You've not heard the last of this," Trensshe said.

"That's as may be."

"When did Kelly leave Rome?"

"Again I don't see that it's any concern of yours. After he and Reynard had had their little talk, obviously. If you want to play the private detective, maybe you should start in the bars in the Piazza. Reynard may have picked up a woman there after Gary came back here. It's just a suggestion, but the most helpful one I can make."

XLII

Tom Durward sat by the open window of the hotel room looking into the dark. The notebook he had bought at a stationer's that afternoon lay on the table behind him. What he wanted to write in it – what he had intended to write when he bought it – couldn't be written. You couldn't, as an accessory to murder, write an analysis of why you had acted as you did. It was too silly to think of. And yet the temptation was extreme. Would he, he wondered, have acted the same way if the dead man hadn't proved to be Reynard Yallett? Perhaps, but his motive would have been different: pity. As it was, to dispose of the corpse and then a day later stop the car, and burn Yallett's passport on a Calabrian hillside: sweet revenge, eaten cold.

He picked up the notebook. There is no need, he wrote, to speak to Stephen Mallany about Jamie. I can write *Finis*.

Then he thought: but my whole life has been corrupted by that first death.

He could not bring himself to write that, though for the moment he believed it to be true. Instead, picking up his pen again, he wrote, "Yet I was already a drunk, priding myself on the courage with which I contemplated the abyss, though in reality – reality? – practised in the habit of evasion. Who among us hasn't known his promised land, his day – days? – of ecstasy and his end in exile. Conrad wrote that somewhere (I think). He is one of the trinity I still return to: Stendhal, Conrad, Proust. As for ... in the Fall Tolstoy was always there but we did not go to him any more."

He pushed away the books, took his stick, let himself out of the hotel, and limped in the direction, again, of the beach.

The moon was up and lay calm on the water. After a bit the beach became stony, and then there were rocks obstructing further progress. Silence enclosed him. He felt good and sat on a rock smoking and watching the moonlight on the sea. They had come as far as was necessary, he thought. He would call Kate in the morning.

He walked higher up the beach on his way back to the town and the hotel. Just below the esplanade there were some benches and one was occupied. He was going to pass by when he saw it was Gary.

"Couldn't sleep," Tom said, statement, not question, and sat beside him.

"I was thinking we might go north again tomorrow. The trip's been long enough to be convincing."

"Me and Dr Sturzo ... there's no point in it," Gary said.

"No," Tom said, "I suppose not, now. So what will you do?"

"Don't know."

"Go home? Back to London?"

"I've killed two," Gary said. "The first, the nigger, didn't set out to do him, you know. Rough him up, make him piss himself, that was ... it got out of hand. And Mr Yallett, he was asking for it like I said, but all I wanted to do was stop him doing what he was doing. Doesn't make sense. None of it makes sense. What you done doesn't make sense."

"Perhaps not. But we did it. Can't be undone."

"No," Gary said. "He'd like to be mates with me, wouldn't he? Erik, the way he looks at me, I don't like it, gives me the creeps. If they question him ... do you think he'd stand up to it, or spill everything?"

Tom said, "I think he's tougher than he looks. We're all in it, you know."

Chapter Forty-Two

He heard Gary sniff. Then, "I'm not going back to London. There's too much there I can't take."

"You're probably right," Tom said. "A clean break. I've been thinking. A friend of mine, a Pole, used to be a stuntman in Hollywood, runs a bar in Lyon. He might give you a job, tide you over for a bit. What do you say? You don't have to answer now. Obviously. Think about it."

"Lyon, that's in France, isn't it?"

The next day they drove north. Tom said he intended to leave the car in Naples. They could take a train from there. He would telephone his Polish friend. Maybe Gary could go straight up to Lyon.

In Naples Erik went to an internet café to check his e-mail. There were several messages from his agent in Los Angeles. There was a part for him if he shifted his ass.

XLIII

Tom spoke to Kate, then to Stefan in Lyon. For Kate it was a kind of solution. It was better in any case that Gary should not return to Rome, oh for several reasons. But what about his passport? And his clothes? He had his passport with him, Tom had checked that; he'd slipped it into his jacket pocket when he went to dress after that shower, showed he was thinking even then, didn't it. As for clothes, they didn't matter, surely. No, Kate said, tell you what. I'll meet him at Termini, he'll have to change trains anyway, with a case. Besides I want to say good-bye to him, owe him that.

Speaking to Stefan, Tom was circumspect. The boy was in trouble, no, not with the police, Stefan needn't worry about that – not that he would much, would he? If Tom remembered him right? So could he accommodate him for a while, as a favour to Tom. Yes, those had been good nights they'd enjoyed, in LA and also down Mexico way. Thanks, do the same for you one day, but there'd be no need for that, now Stefan was so respectable. How's Maria, give her a big hug from me. Thanks, mate, *mon vieux.*

Stephen ... Stefan, Tom thought, like the brackets enfolding what to him was essentially Jamie's story.

Tom said to Erik, "I've bought Gary his ticket. He wants to travel alone. We'd better see him off. What are your plans?"

"It's odd," Erik said, "it feels like the end of a holiday. Or the end of a school term." They took a taxi to the station. It was evident Gary couldn't wait to be rid of them. But he managed to shake hands. When Erik wished him luck, the corner of his mouth moved as if he might attempt a smile.

He said, "Don't suppose we'll meet again, but thanks."

Chapter Forty-Three

The train was filling up. Tom looked at his watch.

"You've got Stefan's address. You'll find he's all right. Give him my best …"

"Do you think he'll be all right?" Erik said as they watched the train pull out.

"It depends what you mean by all right. And you?"

"This part my agent's got me. I booked my flight this morning. From Rome on Friday. It's good."

They were drinking coffee in the station bar. Erik would take the next train to Rome. He said, "Do you think we've got away with it?"

"Who can tell? Hertz will valet the car before they rent it again. They're punctilious about that. Of course there'll be questions asked when they find the body which somebody must do someday, but, well, you'll be in California."

"Yes," Erik said. "If you don't mind me saying so, you've written us a great script."

"Sure," Tom said. "Maybe we should make a movie of it. Maybe not."

"Shame we can't. What are your plans now?"

"Capri for a few days. Most beautiful place I know. Used to be happy there."

"Capri? That's where Tiberius retired to, but not for orgies according to the novel I read. Do you think that was right?"

"Who can tell?" Tom said again. "Most history's fiction. That's what we've been doing the last few days, making a fiction of history."

Erik went to fetch a couple more espressos from the bar.

Tom said: "Douglas, the writer I've been boring you with in Calabria, set a novel on Capri. Its theme, how to make murder acceptable to a bishop."

"Neat," Erik said. "Cool. What's the title?"

"*South Wind.* Dated, but you might enjoy it." He lit a half-cigar. "You'll let Belinda down lightly, won't you. She'll miss you. She's fond of you, more than that maybe. None of my business but ..."

"She's wonderful, Belinda. Don't think I don't know what I owe her. I'll miss her too, but ..."

"Yes," Tom said, "there's always a 'but'."

XLIV

Reynard's disappearance made the English Sundays. There was a long piece by Trensshe, leaning heavily on the connection with Gary Kelly. Was Kelly the last person to see Yallett? Trensshe asked, implying the last to see him alive. A photograph of Gary leaving the Old Bailey amidst jeers from a hostile crowd after his acquittal accompanied Trensshe's story. Clarissa's profile of Yallett, hastily concluded and with a new slant, both questioning and elegiac, was given prominence on the front page of the paper's review section. She too mentioned Gary. "Reynard couldn't get that case out of his head," she wrote, "yet shied away like a nervous thoroughbred when I probed him. Has his obsession with Gary Kelly some connection with his disappearance?" Elsewhere, there was a report of the Home Secretary's intention to review the law on Double Jeopardy ... Even Mike got in on the act, with a piece suggesting that this was not the first time the Italian police, who were, he conceded, overworked and underpaid, had shown a distinct lack of interest in the disappearance of a foreigner.

"It could have been worse," Kate telephoned Belinda to say.

"Oh I never take anything the papers say seriously ..."

Instead she immersed herself in *The Charterhouse*, which she hadn't read since she was sixteen. It was Erik's copy. When she knew he was returning to America, she had gone to the Lion bookshop and bought him a new copy, so that she might inscribe it, and keep his as what? A token? No, more than that. A bond. Now, near the end, when she arrived at a certain sentence in the chapter, "An Evening in Church", she found herself in tears. "The kind of misery which a frustrated love engenders in the soul makes anything that calls for concentration or action a frightful burden." How true that is, she thought, how well Stendhal understood women, even if this sentence was actually written with reference to Fabrizio himself. And I don't even have a photograph of him. Stephen was coming for supper. She could – even might – ask him for one. Or Erik himself to send one? That was better. Their parting had been all the more bitter because he was so excited by the prospect of resuming his career and "this great part my agent has got for me", and she had had to try to share his delight; and reveal nothing of her pain. The most she allowed herself was to say, "Write and let me know how things work out ..." and, at the barrier, "Don't forget me".

But he would. She was sure of that. And why not? He was young. Perhaps in thirty years, when she was dead, and he was ageing badly, his beauty gone, then he might think of her with tenderness. Well, that was it. And if he did write she would be distressed by the banality ... still she would settle for that.

Reynard's story took a new twist in the week that followed. *The Times* ran a half-page on the disappearance. The writer had done some digging. Reynard was deep in debt, especially to the Inland Revenue, on account of his failure to file tax returns for several years. Indeed he was threatened with bankruptcy. He was also due to appear before the Bar Council; there were allegations, unsubstantiated of course, of approaches made to a female member of a jury in a case he was pleading. In short, he might, it was hinted, have had good reason to disappear.

Kate related this to Belinda in some excitement.

Chapter Forty-Four

"No mention of Gary, takes it all well away from us."

But Gary returned in a tabloid later in the week.

"Where is Gary Kelly?" He too, it seemed, had vanished, and here too it was suggested he had last been seen in the company of the man who had defended him, Reynard Yallett – for whom, it was suggested, Interpol were now searching. Reynard Yallett had been married twice and was regularly photographed with top models, stars and posh It-girls. But the tabloid had found "a close friend" to say that it was no secret Reynard swung both ways. His name had been linked with a Premier Division footballer and a member of a Boy Band (now disbanded). Could the disappearance of Reynard Yallett and Gary Kelly be connected? Could it be mere coincidence that both had vanished at the same time? "Reynard has taken several holidays in Thailand," a source revealed.

"Oh, it's too silly," Belinda said, handing the paper back to Kate. "Who can be bothered with such nonsense? Do you suppose anyone takes it seriously? All the same, the more confusion the better, don't you think. I do wonder about the body though."

XLV

In appearance and manner Commissioner Angeloni was as mild as his voice on the telephone had suggested. His dark suit gave the impression of having been cleaned too often and the heels of his polished black shoes were very slightly worn down; but his shirt was freshly ironed and the maroon tie neatly knotted. His complexion was dark and he spoke with the slight lisp characteristic of his home town of Bari. He apologised to Kate for the necessity that brought him here to trouble her, and looked inquiringly at Belinda. Kate introduced them, explaining why she had asked her friend to be with her, and then said she would make coffee.

"You have no idea," the Commissioner said, "how tiresome this sort of business is. You have lived long in Rome, Marchesa?"

"I come and go," Belinda said, "but almost twenty years."

"Then you are closer to being a true Roman than I am myself ..."

He sighed, and said, "Of course, you understand that this is merely a formality, this visit of mine. I must make a report, and, like nineteen out of twenty reports I make, it will contain nothing of significance. As for the twentieth, the significant one, what is its usual fate? Let me tell you: it disappears, it is lost; someone has found something in it embarrassing. This is the story of police work."

He sat on a straight-backed chair, though Kate had indicated a more comfortable one, and he held himself upright, primly even, with his knees together and his dusky long-fingered hands resting one on each thigh.

"Yes," he said, "so much of it is futility. Yet we must observe the formalities. What a charming room this is. And now coffee ..."

Chapter Forty-Five

He stood up and stepped aside to allow Kate to place the tray on the table.

"The work of the police would be impossible without coffee. Indeed coffee is the motor of Italy, is it not?"

"Of modern life, perhaps," Kate said.

"Indeed. How pleasant it would be to sit and talk philosophy with you ladies. Your book, *dottoressa*, on the Belgian Nazi – a masterpiece. I so greatly admired your understanding of the criminal mind which does not recognise itself as criminal, inasmuch as it approves whatever seems rational and necessary at the moment, for the promotion of self-interest. But, alas ... This unfortunate Mr Yallett – but why do I say 'unfortunate' when we do not know what his fortune may be, or may have been? – appears to me a disagreeable creature. Am I wrong?"

"Viewed from certain angles," Kate said, "that would be so. You agree, Bel?"

Belinda thought: what we must do is be careful of our tenses. This man is clever and I have no doubt not half as sympathetic as he appears. She contented herself with nodding her head in agreement.

"I have to say," the Commissioner continued, "that when these two English journalists, whom you no doubt know, first disclosed their concern, indeed their fears, we seemed to be occupied with a trivial matter. People are free to come and go as they please, are they not? This is what it means to be citizens of a liberal democratic Europe, a Europe without frontiers. It is admirable. Which of us would have it otherwise? But it makes police work more difficult. Indeed if it was not for modern technology ... our colleagues in London are inquiring into Mr Yallett's mobile phone records. That may yield something, but I am not hopeful. When intelligent people wish to disappear ... Well, they don't make use of devices so easily checked."

"You think then," Kate said, "that Reynard has simply disappeared, gone off somewhere, of his own accord?"

The commissioner sighed.

"Indeed yes. There is no indication to the contrary. I would be quite happy with that, all the more so because my colleagues in London, and also, as I understand, the Press there, have raised the possibility that he had good reason to do so."

"So it would seem," Belinda said, "if you can believe the newspapers."

"Quite so. However there is another matter, with which, *dottoressa*, I am sorry to trouble you. The question has been raised of the young man, Kelly, who seems also to have disappeared at the same time as Mr Yallett who defended him, it appears, on a charge of murder ..."

"Of which he was acquitted," Kate said. "He had good reason to be grateful to Mr Yallett ..."

"Certainly. But it is the coincidence of his disappearance that is interesting. He was staying here, I am informed."

"Commissioner," Kate said, "you were kind enough to say you liked my book on Klaes Boorkampf. I was intending to write a similar one about Gary Kelly, his case and background. That's why he was staying here. You might like to know that I spent six weeks as lodger in the guest-room of the sanatorium where Dr Boorkampf was confined. I like to get close to my subjects."

"But I understand," he smiled. "I understand perfectly. But the question is – that which I am obliged to try and answer – where is this Gary Kelly now? You see?"

"It didn't work out. There's no book in his story. He was less interesting than I thought."

Belinda lit a cigarette.

"You don't mind, do you?" she said. "Or do you smoke yourself? I should have asked. You do? Good."

She leaned forward to offer him one and then her lighter. His eyes were soft, long-suffering, gentle as a spaniel's.

She said, "But the papers have it wrong. Forgive me for butting in as it were, but there is no coincidental disappearance. We don't know what happened to Reynard Yallett, but Gary didn't go off with him as they suggest. That's nonsense. When Kate decided that there wasn't going to be a book – it was a friendly decision, wasn't it, Kate – Gary then went off south with two friends of ours, just for a few days."

"So has the young man returned to Rome?"

"Well, no," Kate said, "there would be no point."

"So where is he now?"

"I don't know exactly," Kate said. "Either in France or back in England, I suppose."

The commissioner frowned again. There was a long silence, broken only by the noise of the traffic from the avenue below.

Kate said, "I didn't mention this to the journalists who asked me about him, because, well, in the first place, I see no reason why he should be bothered by them, and, secondly, I took a considerable dislike to Mr Trensshe."

"I also," Angeloni said. "Not a sympathetic type ... These friends of yours? They have returned to Rome?"

"Well, no," Belinda said. "Erik who's a young American is back in the States. He's an actor, and his agent had got him a part. And Tom Durward said he

186

was going to spend a few days or weeks, I don't know, on Capri. It was Capri, wasn't it, Kate, not Ischia?"

"No, Capri."

"Admirable. My colleagues there can speak with him. Not that it is of any importance that they should. Nevertheless ... And, *dottoressa*, you didn't see Mr Yallett after lunch on the Saturday. That is correct? Good. As I say, I regret to have had to trouble you with these formalities. Nevertheless it has been for me a pleasure to meet you both."

He opened his briefcase, and produced a copy of the Italian edition of Kate's book on Boorkampf.

"Perhaps you would be so kind as to sign this for me, *dottoressa*?"

"A nice man," Belinda said, "but also, I think, a clever one. I hope I was right to play the Tom and Erik card."

"Oh yes, we had to. Do you think he'll think it odd we hadn't – or I hadn't – played it before?"

"Why should he? Why should you have? His was the first official enquiry after all."

"That's true. We'd better warn Tom to expect a visit ..."

"Yes, but ..." Belinda said, "perhaps not from your phone or even mine. I liked the commissioner, but he's clever, I think. And a policeman."

"Yes," Kate said. "You can never be sure what they believe and what they don't. And, from my observation, the sympathetic ones are the most sceptical."

XLVI

At thirty, Camus wrote, a man should know himself like the palm of his hand ... know how far he can go, foretell his failures – be what he is. Fair enough, Durward thought, but uncertainty returns with the years. What they had done couldn't have been foretold, what he had done anyway, couldn't speak for the others.

He might spend the winter on Capri. Why not? He had never done so. On his first visit in his Douglas period they had discovered and penetrated a subterranean *vinaio* frequented by old men who had been boys together on the island. All dead now, he supposed, and in any case *vinai* were denied him; but he had found it *simpatico* in those days. Two of the old men had been pall-bearers at Douglas's funeral.

Three letters had arrived that morning. He had stuffed them into his pocket; it was years since he had torn open an envelope on receipt. Now he called for another coffee, got his cigar going, and slid his thumb under the flap of the first, Belinda's.

"It's absurd," she wrote, "that one hesitates to put things on paper, and yet one does. I suppose that's evidence of guilt which however is far from what I feel. So I just wanted to say thank you and it does seem you have managed brilliantly. There's so much to say, but it can wait till you return to Rome."

The second letter was from Erik:

> Dear Tom, it feels kind of strange to be writing a letter that I can't e-mail. I wanted to say it was a great experience getting the chance to know you a little, though maybe it's not so little considering everything. My agent told me I'd grown up! So maybe something shows. My part's a real good one. I play a young psychotic killer! Kills his father actually! I had to laugh remembering you

saying 'happy as the boy who's killed his father', didn't you say it was a German proverb or something. I wonder how Gary is making out with your Polish friend. Do you think we'll ever see or hear from him again? I guess not. I never did find anything I could speak to him about, though I wanted to. But I guess I'll play this part as if I was Gary, what do you think? I don't know how to end this, so I'll just say, Love, Erik.

P.S. *Gehenna*'s out on video and I watched it again yesterday. What a movie!! And I've finished *The Charterhouse*. Quel novel!! Che romanzo!! Maybe you should write our one.

Tom pictured the boy knitting his brows and licking his lip with a quick nervous gesture as he wondered how much he could dare write and so give himself away.

The third was from Stephen Mallany:

Dear Mr Durward,

Belinda kindly gave me your address. I'm sorry I was out of things while you were in Rome, and I gather from her and Meg that I have you to thank for what I can only call my deliverance. I shudder to think of what might have become of me if you hadn't acted the Good Samaritan.

I think you remember who I am and even, or especially, a letter I wrote to you many years ago.

We have, I believe, two things in common even apart from alcoholism. (In that context I may say that I recognised you that evening you arrived at our meeting, and then I fled in terror and guilt.)

These two things are, I believe, that we both loved Jamie and have both held ourselves responsible in some obscure fashion for his death. I know I have; I let him down.

Besides thanking you, there are two reasons why I now write – I all but wrote, didn't dare to write, and perhaps should have done so.

Chapter Forty-Six

The newspapers have been full of stories about the disappearance of that terrible man, Reynard Yallett, and this gives me the courage to say what I lacked the courage to write almost twenty years ago: that Yallett was indeed the prefect I spoke of then who forced himself on Jamie and left him consumed with self-disgust and a deep sense of humiliation.

It is a terrible thing for a priest to write but I could wish that the suggestions made, obliquely, in some of the newspapers that Yallett may have taken his own life were true. I can't believe them. The life-force of evil is so powerful. But if he has, then justice is served. The Lord is not mocked.

I do not think you will wish to see me to speak of these things, which is another reason why I write. And in any case I do not believe I would have the courage to engage you in conversation.

Emerging from this last appalling bout has left me trembling and fearful as I try to look reality in the face. But you will know all about that.

Please do not feel the need to reply to this letter. That would only embarrass us both. But if I am still in Rome when you return here, I hope we may meet and exchange those civil nothings which enable us to skate over the thin ice that covers the abyss.

Belinda and Meg have been wonderful to me, but both have their own cross to bear, and Belinda is, I fear, unhappy as I have never known her. God grant us the serenity to accept the things we cannot change – that is, our fundamental nature.

Yours sincerely,
Stephen Mallany.

So there it was.

Earlier that morning he had had the interview which Kate had warned him of with the local police. Yes, he had said, the young man Kelly had come south with him and another friend; yes, another

190

young friend. Yes, it had been a sudden decision; but why not? The idea had come up, when he had been speaking enthusiastically of a visit he had made to Calabria many years ago. They had none of them any obligations, and acting on impulse was pleasing, was it not? Indeed yes. And the young man Kelly? He had last seen him off on a train for France. No, he had no address for him. And the young American? Back in California, working. Il signor Durward was in the movie business himself? Had been, was now retired, more or less, inasmuch as a writer ever retires. The conversation was friendly. They drank coffee. Tom gave the policeman a cigar. These enquiries were routine, Signor Durward would understand. Indeed yes, again, formalities were necessary if tiresome.

And that was perhaps that.

He sat, idle, under a trellis of roses in flower, and, looking down and over to his left, his eyes feasted on the deep restfulness of the sea. Gleams of light shone reflected from its mirror-like expanse. Then, in the hour before sunset, he would stroll to the Arco Naturale, through which you see the long arm of the mainland by Sorrento swathed in a pale dying blue. Peace, he thought. Vengeance is mine, proclaimed Yahweh who liked to keep the best to himself. But Durward had enjoyed the dish too, eaten cold, as the Sicilian proverb recommends, and savoured.

XLVII

For weeks Reynard Yallett lay undisturbed. Undisturbed by men, women, or children, that is. Crows picked out his blue eyes. Scavenging dogs tore at his flesh. The rains of autumn washed the blood away. The little stream by which the body had come to a halt in its descent rose fast and high and poured over him. The waters subsided and it was then that two ten year-old boys, Aldo and Peppino, playing truant from school, wandering at random and looking for a quiet place to smoke, came upon it. The sight alarmed them. They gathered branches, tearing off bushes and covered it up, then piled stones on top. It was another two weeks before Peppino started having nightmares, and these recurred so often, waking his mother with screams, that she questioned him diligently in an attempt to discover what it was that had so affected him. "You've always been such a calm happy child," she said. "And now?" Even so it was Christmas before he confessed what he and Aldo had found and what they had done.

So his father and elder brother went in search of the body, but they looked in the wrong place, for the boy's directions had been vague; and came on nothing.

"He's imagining it," the father said; and was relieved, not only because he thought this true, but because he had not wanted to find the body of which his son had whimperingly spoken. Such things spelled trouble.

Accordingly it lay there, decomposing, throughout the winter.

XLVIII

"With leaden foot Time creeps along
While Delia is away:
With her, nor plaintive was the song,
Nor tedious was the day ..."

Yes, indeed: for Delia read Erik, and the poet's first two lines were hers ... with leaden foot. He spoke for her, this Richard Jago, a friend according to her Concise DNB – though how she had come into possession of these three volumes she couldn't recall – of Shenstone and Somerville, and also, not surprisingly, a vicar. The following lines were less accurate. Erik's tune was often plaintive, and no doubt there was a certain tedium in days of his company, days which nevertheless she wished restored to her.

It was ridiculous to think of him so often, so long and longingly to picture him leaning against the terrace wall or stretched in her bed with the sheet half-tangled round him. Ridiculous too to spend hours poring over her old Oxford Book of English verse, her sad father's copy, the Quiller-Couch version. But there it was, she did. There she was, as Johnson remarked on the opposite page: "condemn'd to Hope's delusive mine ... our social comforts drop away." Could Erik be described as a social comfort? Well, yes, perhaps; what else was love, her sort of love anyway, but that?

She wrote to him often, sent the letters but rarely, and then much amended, keeping the tone light, anything expressive of her yearning excised. When he replied, which he did, twice, the naivety with which he wrote made her feel the hollowness of her love and yet also its sharpness.

He said nothing of what she wanted to know: who was sharing his bed? She couldn't believe he slept alone. When in the second letter he assured her that he would never forget her, she took that as signifying that he never expected to see her again, and assumed that even their barren correspondence would wither. But perhaps he didn't see it as barren: that was her word, after all.

One day, in Stephen's apartment, while he was in the kitchen making tea, she abstracted a photograph of the boy, slipping it into her bag. It showed him in an armchair, his head resting against flowered chintz. His lips were parted as if awaiting a kiss. His white T-shirt was rucked up in soft folds. She imagined the flat belly it concealed. At night she languished over the photograph, absurdly.

There were few people that autumn whose company did not irritate her. She spent more hours in the French church before the Caravaggios than in conversation with others. She understood now more than ever St Matthew's reluctance and the incredulity of those he had been with, when Christ called him.

She still attended meetings, not sure why. Was it her imagination or did the others there now look at her with concern? It wasn't entirely imagination, for one evening Bridget whispered, "Are you sure you're all right? You don't look yourself, you know."

"It's nothing," she said, "really nothing, nothing to worry about anyway."

Kate left for her conference in Geneva.

"We have to keep going," she said to Belinda.

"Oh, absolutely."

But something in their old easy intimacy was broken. She found herself blaming Kate for Erik's departure. His share of their action had in some way liberated him. She ought, of course, to be glad of that – for his sake; would be if she loved him truly as a person, instead of what? "A toy" was the nasty word that came reproachfully to mind. Gary, she thought, gave him something, though I don't know what.

She spent more time with Stephen because they had had at least Erik in common, not that they talked of him except when once Stephen said, "I never want to be like that with anyone again. He was my last infatuation. I hope so anyway." She had no answer for that.

One day Stephen said, "I've made such a mess of my life, you know."

They were in his apartment which was now neat, clean, and tidy, stripped of all evidence of the horrors he had endured there. She picked up the book he had been reading and had laid aside when she arrived. It was Law's *Serious Call to a Devout and Holy Life*.

"Yes," he said, taking it from her. "You know what Johnson said of this: it was the book that gave him 'the first occasion of thinking in earnest of religion'. Considering I'm a priest I've come to it rather late. Nevertheless ... I've been off my head, you know, all my life I sometimes think. You're the only person here I can talk to about this, Belinda."

"I don't know. I should have thought I was one of the last people. It's something I just don't understand. It says nothing to me."

"I've found myself able to pray again," he said. "Things have come together since my last bout. Something's been released in me. It's connected with Tom Durward."

"I'm sorry, Stephen, you've lost me."

"What do you think has happened to Reynard Yallett?" he said, and then, without giving her time to reply, continued, "I was out of course when he was here in Rome and then disappeared, but I've read the stuff in the newspapers. Do you know, when I was coming out of that bout and having nightmares, as one does – you know – I was sure I had killed him. I saw myself sticking a knife in his gut, and the blood spouting over me. Can you imagine? Of course, I had killed him often enough in my mind."

"I don't understand," she said, again. "What makes you think he is dead, and how did you know him? I didn't know that you did or that he meant anything to you."

"Oh yes," he said, "he meant too much to me, but now – don't ask me why because I don't know – I am free of him."

"But you don't really think you've killed him? I mean, you know you didn't, don't you? You've no reason even to think he's dead."

"It doesn't matter now, that's the great thing. I've been released, it's an answer to prayer. But I am a murderer by intention, only I never had the courage, if that's what was lacking, to be one in practice."

"You'd better tell," she said.

So he did, stumbling at first, embarrassed, confessing more fully than he ever had at meetings, telling her of the fear that Yallett had inspired in him, of his love for Jamie. "You mean, Tom Durward's nephew?" Belinda said, pieces beginning to fit ...

"Yes, I often think all the boys I've ever loved have been no more than substitutes, quite inadequate substitutes, for what I lost when he killed himself. And yet I never laid a hand on him, it was Yallett did that, and more ..."

Belinda's thought was: that probably meant nothing to Reynard; these things didn't, I'm sure. Once he'd had his way, that was that.

She said, "Do you think though he felt guilty when the boy killed himself, drowning, wasn't it?"

Stephen lifted his head. Telling his story had brought tears to his eyes.

Now he said, "Do you know I've never thought of that, never considered how he may have felt. I hated him too much. And I hated myself because I had done nothing ... nothing, either way."

That was all. The conversation had to stop there. They were in danger of entering intolerable territory.

Stephen said, "I owe you a lot, Bel, but this life's too much for me. I'm getting out, leaving Rome, going back to England. I can't manage on my own, I know that now, and AA's not enough, when there's sex, my sort of sex, as well as drink to contend with, or better, escape from. So I've applied to join the Community of the Paraclete ..."

"I've never heard of it, I'm afraid. Paraclete? That's the Holy Ghost, isn't it?"

"Yes, it's an order of monks, an Anglican one, very small, they have only one House, in the Yorkshire dales, but they've accepted me as a novice. Do you think I've made the right decision?"

"Stephen, how can I possibly tell? I know nothing of these matters. But perhaps yes ... I don't know."

"You do know I'm no good at being on my own though?"

"Yes, I know that," she said.

XLIX

In Geneva Kate resisted the urge to take a train to Lyon to look up Gary in the Polish restaurant Tom had given her the address of. The temptation had been strong. She was still curious. She also felt a responsibility towards him and, as before leaving Rome she had admitted to Belinda, something strangely like affection. "And of course I failed him," she said, which she could see irritated Belinda, who made no reply. Now, walking by the lake wrapped up and wearing a fur hat against the sharp wind from the mountains, she told herself it would be self-indulgence and, if he was settled there, disturbing for him. Perhaps, she thought, I'll go instead to talk with his mother in London; I think she liked me, not that that matters.

London was chill, wet, miserable. You were conscious of the crowd there as never in Rome, conscious on account, she thought, of pent-up frustrations all around you, even aggression. Still she had to talk with her agent who took her for lunch in her club in Soho. The agent, a young woman called Hilary who wore steel-rimmed spectacles and was celebrated, locally, for her ability to put publishers in their place and her authors, often, in places where they had no wish to be, urged Kate to strike out on a new line.

"You were," she said, "the last person to see Reynard Yallett before his disappearance. I want you to write a book about it."

"But I know nothing," Kate said.

"No matter. He'd been living a double life for years. That's right up your street."

She expanded on the subject at length, over several Daiquiris which she drank throughout the meal of crab dressed with a pineapple coulis. Mineral water, she said parenthetically, forgetting what Kate was drinking, was so last year. Reynard, she said, was the coming fashion, he had overleapt the "new man". He was a real shit, you must do him, she said.

"You make him sound like a Simon Raven character," Kate said.

"Simon who?"

She was a very up-to-the-minute agent, Kate thought, so "with it" – if "with it" wasn't obsolete – that only the now concerned her.

"I'll think about it," she said, meaning she wouldn't, and regretting her former agent who had transferred her to Hilary on his withdrawal to the Dordogne.

Hilary stubbed out her Marlboro Light in the coulis. "Clarissa will bring you up to speed. The girl's so now she's the new black and always late. But she adored Reynard. She adores you too. So she says."

She arrived with the coffee, all legs and liberty, lavish with kisses and short on apologies. She was delighted, she said – "entranced" was her actual word – that Kate was going to write about Reynard.

"Philip's certain he's dead. He just knows that Gary Kelly killed him. That's what he says. Of course he's obsessed with Gary, he was the great success of his career, the utter zenith."

"Yes," Kate said, "I remarked the obsession."

"It's crazy," Clarissa said. "Reynard's not dead, I would know if he was, I would feel it here." She fluttered her fingers over her small breasts. "Besides he's been seen in Buenos Aires, he's always had a thing about Latin America. I mean, you can't see Reynard letting those little shits at the Inland Revenue and the Bar Council get on top of him, can you? No, Philip's right off the wall, he's a monomaniac, which is only part of the reason we've split up. I'm with Mike now, did you know that? But you did know he had left

Meg, didn't you? He says it's because she understood him; he's so funny, Mike. Oh he sends you love, he's in great form. We've taken him on staff, you know. It's what he's been needing, he says, and he really is brill."

"Is he drinking?" Kate said.

"He wouldn't be Mike if he wasn't, would he?"

"No, I suppose not," Kate said. "And what of Philip, how's he taken it?"

"Do you know he's hardly noticed. Like I said, he's obsessed only with Gary Kelly. He says he has evidence that he's engaged in the smuggling of illegal immigrants. Do you think that's likely?"

"No," Kate said, "not at all," having actually no idea.

L

It was Sol's custom to give a party on Christmas Eve for all the members of the AA group still in Rome, and for their families and any visiting guests.

"Do you mind?" Belinda said to her sort of brother-in-law, Kenneth, and his wife Maura, who had arrived the day before. "You can get out of it easily. You're not house-guests as Sol puts it," for at Maura's insistence they were staying in a hotel, the Inghilterra, rather than with Belinda.

Kenneth looked at Maura.

"Why should we want to get out of it?" she said. "I take it there is booze for us unregenerates."

"Good. I'll call for you at seven. Sol and Amelia's apartment is just round the corner from you, in Largo Goldoni."

She got there on time. Kenneth was waiting in the foyer.

"Maura's running late," he said. "She spent the afternoon shopping. I rather think she hoped you might be late yourself."

"Well, yes, I usually am, aren't I?"

"And now you're not. Is there something you want to talk about?"

"Not precisely, but it's good to see you."

"Likewise. Will Kate be at this do?"

"No," Belinda said, "she's away. In fact she's in Aberdeen for Christmas, with her parents. Her father's been far from well."

"Pity. I like Kate. I'm told she's writing a book about Reynard Yallett now."

"I don't think so."

"That's the word anyway. You were nearly engaged to him once, weren't you, Bel?"

"A long time ago and in another country. For my sins."

"Maura was his pupil in chambers, you know, for a bit. Before we knew each other. No happy memories there either."

"Why should you suppose Kate is writing about him?"

"Well, that's the word, as I say."

"Far as I know it's nonsense. I mean, why should she? Why indeed should anyone want a book about him?"

"You do live out of things, don't you? His vanishing act has been the talk of the town."

"Small town then," Belinda said.

"Granted. But it's a mystery, everybody loves a mystery."

"Not me. Reynard can be in Thailand or Cuba or at the bottom of the sea for all I care ..."

"Some think he's dead. Philip Trensshe is putting it about that he's been murdered, by the boy Kelly."

"Sounds crazy," Belinda said. "What possible motive could Gary have had? Reynard defended him successfully, didn't he?"

"Yes indeed, but now Kelly seems to have disappeared too ... Others think they've gone off together, as a couple. That seem likely? You met Kelly, I assume, when he was here with Kate. Well, I know you did because you were interested enough to get me to send you the reports of his trial. What did you make of him?"

"Just a boy," Belinda said, "a rather sad boy. He might be likeable if he allowed anyone close enough to like him."

"Ah, here comes Maura ..."

Sol and Amelia's hospitality was lavish. There was a huge, a towering, macaroni pie, with chicken livers, hard-boiled eggs, strips of ham, chicken and truffles, embedded in masses of glistening macaroni, the dish kept piping hot by being placed on an electric thermostatically-controlled ring. There were two turkeys and a pumpkin pie, a York ham and a swordfish surrounded by prawns, a Caesar salad and a potato salad and tomato salad. Since non-drinking alcoholics mostly recover the sweet tooth of childhood, Amelia provided them with a king-size Monte Bianco cake, dripping with cream, English trifles, apple and cherry pies and a *torta di ricotta*, behind which was arranged on an ashet a mountain of fruit so beautifully and painterly balanced that it seemed a sin to disturb it. There was mineral water, and Coca-Cola, and elderflower cordial and lime juice, and for the unregenerate, as Maura had called them, bottles of Marino wine from the Castelli and two-litre flasks of Chianti.

"It's marvellous," Belinda said, "I don't know how you do it."

"We'll be broke for weeks, we always are after Christmas," Amelia said, "but it's worth it."

"We miss Kate," Sol said, "any word of her father?"

"Much the same, I believe."

"And Stephen? Do you think he's made the right decision?"

"Who can tell? What was here wasn't working for him."

What isn't here isn't working for me, she thought, smiling however to see Fergus take Maura by the arm, an Irishman to Irish girl, and hear him quiz her about Galway.

"I'm a Limerick man meself," he said in his hoarse breathy voice, "and what wouldn't I give to be back there with a pint of porter before me? But you can't turn back the clock, can you? And now I'm on the road to understanding myself and why I drink, I'm happy to be sober. And I couldn't be sober back home, things would be too strong for me there. I'm a soft man, m'dear ..."

Kenneth was kneeling beside Bridget who sat in a corner, not liking being there, but having come, as she'd told Belinda every Christmas Eve for the last four years, because it would have been cowardly to keep away and, besides, Tomaso thought it was good for her. Indeed he insisted. Kenneth was kneeling because there was no other way in which he might hear Bridget's whispering, and she was looking over his shoulder at Tomaso who was engaged in conversation with the middle one of Sol's beautiful daughters, Mandy. He was setting himself to charm her but, Belinda knew, Bridget would let it go only so far. Tomaso bullied her, certainly – for her own good of course – but it was still Bridget who wrote the cheques.

To her surprise she saw Tom Durward limp towards her. She hadn't noticed him arrive. "I didn't know you were back in Rome."

"Only arrived this afternoon. Hadn't meant to come."

"There's nothing wrong?"

"Not that I know of."

"How was Capri?"

"Cold and wet when I left."

"I almost came to see you. It's years since I've been there."

"You should have. I'd have liked that."

"Oh I'm always almost doing things ..."

She looked around. The party was gaining in animation. She gestured to Tom and they withdrew into an alcove.

"Your disposal," she said, "seems to have been remarkably effective."

"Just luck."

"Kate had another visit from Commissario Angeloni before she left. They're convinced Reynard left Italy on a false passport. They'd been concerned that his name didn't appear on any of the flight manifests, though he could have gone by train of course, but Scotland Yard or Special Branch, I don't know which, believe he had acquired a false passport and was making plans to vanish. There had been big money transfers, and he had anyway numbered accounts in various offshore whatever they are. Isn't it extraordinary?"

"Just luck," Tom said again. "Gary's walked out on my Polish friend. Without leaving an address, naturally. He may be back in England. Who knows?"

"Does it matter?"

"Can't see that it does."

Tom lit a cigar.

"Despite everything, not such a bad kid. Or is that sentimental?"

"Probably," Belinda said. And what about the other kid, have you heard from him, she wanted to ask, but didn't.

Instead she said, "Stephen's gone into a monastery, did you know that? Stephen Mallany, I mean."

"No," he said. "Can't say I'm surprised though. Maybe Gary has too. Good Catholic boy, you know."

"Doesn't seem likely."

"No, doesn't."

"And Mike and Meg have split," she said.

"Yes, Meg called me. She's gone to New York ..."

Sol knocked a spoon against a glass to obtain silence. "I'm not going to make a speech," he said. "Amelia's forbidden it. She says I can keep my speeches for meetings. So I'm just going to say how good

205

it is to be approaching Christmas sober and to have all but got through another year. It's a joy to see you all here, and so I wish you a merry Christmas and propose we drink a toast to that and to absent friends. Merry Christmas and absent friends ..."

Later they went, most of them, to the Church of Santa Maria in Aracoeli for Midnight Mass. It was full of women in fur coats and beautifully dressed men. Kisses and greetings were exchanged, with loud exclamations, while the priest muttered his way through the sacrament.

When they emerged from the church it was very cold and a piper, dressed as a shepherd from the Abruzzi, played "Silent Night". He probably wasn't a shepherd and hadn't descended from the mountains, but it was a very beautiful moment and good to think he might be.

Belinda's mobile rang.

"Hi, it's me, Erik. Happy Christmas. Have I got the time right? Is it Christmas yet in Roma?"

"Yes, indeed, and Happy Christmas to you. Where are you?"

"On the Coast. On a beach actually, at a party. Where are you?"

"Just coming down the steps from the Aracoeli. It's sweet of you to call."

"Have you been thinking about me?"

"From time to time, quite often really."

"Miss me?"

All around her were people embracing, kissing on both cheeks, hugging, wishing each other good fortune, and below cars roared past, hooting, towards the river or the Aventino.

"Yes," she said, "yes."

"Oh good, I hoped you'd say that. I might come to Roma in the Spring, what do you say?"

"What do you think? I'll look forward to it."

"Must ring off. Love to all."

"Love."

Love to you.

She turned and found Tom Durward by her side.

"That was Erik, he seems all right."

Silently, he accompanied her towards the ghetto and her apartment. They paused in Piazza Mattei by the fountain of the tortoises, and Belinda let her hand slide over the stone thigh of one of the boys holding up a tortoise to drink. They turned into the Via Portico d' Ottavia.

Durward said, "That bar on the corner there … I told you I once stayed with a friend in this street. One morning Jules and I sat outside that bar, we'd come from Spoleto on the night train. We'd gone there for the festival, a bad trip, and on the train back there was an old woman with a hen on a string … straight out of *Under the Volcano* she was. We were both drunks already and addicted to Malcolm Lowry. So we sat outside that bar for hours – is this boring you? No? – talking Lowry, and coming back always to that phrase that runs through the novel, about the church for the bereaved: she is the virgin for those who have nobody with …"

"The Virgin for those who have nobody with … I like that. It's so odd they've never found the body …"

"Call it providence. Perhaps we've survived …"

"The virgin for those who have nobody with …," she leaned up and kissed Durward on the cheek. "We've a lot to be thankful for. Merry Christmas, Tom."

"Merry Christmas …"

He watched her into the house and stood there for a couple of minutes before he moved away in the direction of Largo Argentina. They were both those who had nobody with, but that's how it was. He lit a cigar. It had come to him several times on Capri to make something of what they had been through, even a novel. He knew its first line: "You're mad, Belinda said, you really are, out of your head ..."

But it couldn't be written, and not just because the story couldn't be told, not now, not while any of them were alive. He didn't know enough. He couldn't imagine enough. He couldn't even imagine that telephone conversation between Belinda and Erik. And what would they have said when they were alone together? It was beyond him, just as it had been beyond him to imagine what went on in Gary's head. All he knew were externals ...

Except ... he knew himself, didn't he? The story as it had been seen and experienced by him?

He drew deep on his *toscano*.

Greif zur Feder, Kumpel ...

Perhaps ... perhaps not.

"Nobody go there. Only those who have nobody with ..."

FINIS

Other Vagabonds   Other Vagabonds   Other Vagabonds

Allan Cameron's *In Praise of the Garrulous*

About the book

This first work of non-fiction by the author of *The Golden Menagerie* and *The Berlusconi Bonus*, has an accessible and conversational tone, which perhaps disguises its enormous ambition. The writer examines the history of language and how it has been affected by technology, primarily writing and printing. This leads to some important questions concerning the "ecology" of language, and how any degradation it suffers might affect "not only our competence in organising ourselves socially and politically, but also our inner selves."

Comments

"A deeply reflective, extraordinarily wide-ranging meditation on the nature of language, infused in its every phrase by a passionate humanism" – Terry Eagleton

"This is a brilliant tour de force, in space and in time, into the origins of language, speech and the word. ... Such a journey into the world of the word needs an articulate and eloquent guide: Allan Cameron is both and much more than that." – Ilan Pappé

I like *In Praise of the Garrulous* very much indeed, not only because it says a good many interesting and true things, but because of its *tone* and style. Its combination of personal passion, observation, stories, poetic bits and serious expert argument, expressed as it is in the prose of an intelligent conversation: all this is ideal for holding and persuading intelligent but non-expert readers. In my opinion he has done nothing better." – Eric Hobsbawm.

Price: £8.00   ISBN: 978-0-9560560-0-9   In print

Luciano Mecacci's **Freudian Slips. The casualties of psychoanalysis from the Wolf Man to Marilyn Monroe**

About the book

This is a story of insane pretensions and tragic outcomes. A small cosmopolitan group invented a lifestyle based on self-obsession which to some extent would much later become a mass phenomenon, and no one can challenge the enormous influence of Freud's ideas on Europe's art, writing and wider culture throughout most of the twentieth century.

Never before has the history of psychoanalysis been told with such directness and clarity. Luciano Mecacci's dispassionate examination of where "scientific" ideas can lead when there is a failure of proper scientific rigour has lessons for us today that go far beyond the field of psychology. On the other hand, we should not be too dismissive of Freud the innovative thinker, who perhaps still has something to tell us. Mecacci quotes the great Italian novelist, Italo Svevo, in the prelims to this book: "This Freud of ours is a great man, but more for novelists than for the sick."

Comments

"Mecacci depicts the situations that emerged around the psychoanalyst as a type, with detachment and without prejudice or self-righteousness. His tone is never emphatic and always only documentary, as though he were filming them." – Alessandro Pagnini in *Il Sole 24 Ore*

"Amusing, stimulating, arguable," – *La Stampa*

Price: £10.00   ISBN: 978-0-9560560-1-6   In print

www.vagabondvoices.co.uk

Allan Cameron's **Presbyopia**

About the book

Cameron's collection of bilingual poetry is introduced by an essay on the distinction between myopic and presbyopic poetry: the former focuses on the self, its emotions and its immediate vicinity, while the latter focuses on what is distant in space and time. Poetic myopia is not as negative as the name might imply, nor presbyopia the only desirable form of poetry, but now that two centuries have passed since Wordsworth, whom Heaney has described as the "an indispensable figure in the evolution of modern writing, a finder and keeper of the self-as-subject", the time has perhaps come to put aside our prejudices against the presbyopic – which to some extent resembles the classical or what Nietzsche called the Appolonian, whose attributes are reason, culture, harmony and restraint. Rightly or wrongly these also imply a degree of coldness, a lack of passion and a detachment which today appear the absolute antithesis of poetry.

In reality, all poetry reflects a mixture of the two, and Cameron's poetry is no exception. He writes on politics and philosophy, but always with the passion that comes from a humanist sensitivity.

Price: £12.00   ISBN: 978-0-9560560-3-0   Publication date: 22.09.09